The Further Adventures of Doctor Syn

© 2013
Cover © Canstockphoto/Jurassic

Black Curtain Press
PO Box 632
Floyd VA 24091

ISBN 10: 1-51542-643-2
ISBN 13: 978-1-5154-2643-1

First Edition
10 9 8 7 6 5 4 3 2 1

The Further Adventures of Doctor Syn

Russell Thorndyke

I dedicate the adventures to J.H. CRANE in gratitude for his long and valued friendship to Doctor Syn and myself.

Foreword

This book deals with Doctor Syn's smuggling adventures when his Nightriders were at the height of their success, and although complete in itself, follows chronologically the events recorded in Doctor Syn Returns. "Death to the Scarecrow" is once again the slogan of the authorities, who are ranged against him. The Navy, the Army, Customs Officers, Magistrates, Bow Street Runners, Press-gang and "Informers" are all enlisted to put down the scandalous contraband running on Romney Marsh, and a large reward is offered for the capture, alive or dead, of the mysterious leader.

Chapter 1. Slippery Sam's

On a wild wet November night in the year of grace 1776, a great lumbering coach creaked, squealed and groaned as its steaming team was lashed at top speed along that bleak country road known as Stone Street, which runs, as straight as the Romans built it, between Canterbury and Lympne.

Although an ancient vehicle, the mud-spattered panels of the coach doors were emblazoned with the armorial bearings of His Grace the Archbishop of Canterbury, whose August person was being sadly shaken about inside. His equally distinguished companion was bumping against him with every jolt of the coach. This was General Troubridge of the Dragoons, who sat opposite to his confidential officer, the handsome Major Faunce. These three gentlemen were journeying to Lympne Castle to be guests of Sir Henry Pembury, Justice of the Peace.

It was a Saturday night, and the Archbishop was to deliver an address at the Castle Church in the morning, and then at Evensong go down to Dymchurch to preach, for the Dean of the Peculiars of Romney Marsh, Doctor Syn.

Although the rotund figure of the General was occupying more than his share of the seat, and much to the discomfort of the Archbishop, His Grace was nevertheless glad of his company. The red coats and heavy sabres lent a security which the wild night might well have disturbed, especially as the coach was nearing Slippery Sam's, a lonely farm-house, rumoured to be one of the rallying-places of the Scarecrow, leader of the dreaded Romney Marsh Night-riders.

Although it was only nine o'clock, the coachman noted that all the farmhouse lights were out, and conjectured that Slippery Sam and his wild companions were abed. The guard, however, was better informed. Many a guinea had come his way, during his service under the Archbishop, by doing no more than pass messages along the roads with the Scarecrow's orders. He had never met the Scarecrow. Not that he would have been much wiser if he had, for no one knew the real identity of the Night-riders' ingenious leader. That is, no one but Mipps, the Dymchurch sexton, and the redoubtable Jimmie Bone, gentleman of the road.

These two, and these two only, could have turned King's Evidence against their leader, and gained the reward which the various authorities offered for his capture, alive or dead.

But the Scarecrow had no fear of them. He knew his men, and trusted these two implicitly. The rest of the many hundreds of men who took active part in contraband running knew only that the superhuman being who rode Romney Marsh at night in the guise of a Scarecrow never failed his followers and kept not only their pockets well lined with guineas, but their necks safe from the hangman's noose.

With his top-coat collar turned up and his back to the horses and the driving rain, the guard prepared to earn his illicit guinea. He drew from his deep pocket a flat billet of wood. The queer notches cut into its surface meant nothing to him, but, as the Canterbury landlord of the Rising Sun had explained when he had handed it across the bar: "Slippery Sam will understand. All you have to do is throw it over his hedge." A guinea easily earned, since he had to ride through the storm on the chilly back box in the ordinary course of duty. He turned towards the black line of hedge that ran along on the right of the coach, and which marked the beginning of the farm fields. He watched the twig tops bending with the wind. Soon there would be a break, marking the entrance of the farm lane. Then the hedge would appear again, and then he must throw the queer wooden message. The only thing to guard against was that his action should not attract the notice of the coachman. But that old worthy had enough to occupy his attention. He disliked the vicinity of Slippery Sam's, and was determined to pass it at a full-stretched gallop.

Meanwhile, some dozen men sat silently smoking and drinking in the darkest back kitchen of the farm-house. Not a word was spoken, for everyone was listening. Now and again Sam himself would tiptoe about the room, to fill up his guests' glasses or tankards. A weird figure, Slippery Sam, as he moved about the large kitchen only made the darker by the red glow from the great hearth. A tall middle-aged man with a bald head and a squint. Sometimes he would creep to the steep stairs in the corner and whisper, "Eh, wife?" when a hard female voice would answer, "Nothing." At last, however, this reply was changed to: "Yes. Lights." All the men got to their feet, while Sam, pulling a piece of sacking that draped his shoulders over his head to guard against the driving rain, opened the back door and slithered out silently into the storm.

He found that his wife, who had been watching Stone Street from an attic window, was right. He could see the coach lamps moving rapidly towards him, as he crouched down to wait behind the hedge. And it was the right coach too; the one they were expecting.It was yet too early for the mail, although the coachman, old George, had a confounded habit of making quicker time in bad weather in order to get his outside the drier and his inside the wetter in the Red Lion of Hythe. But the mail horn always rang out as they topped the near rise, and many a warning had Sam received in this way from his friend the guard. If certain notes were played, he knew that the Scarecrow's Night-riders were "out". Other notes would convey that the Excise men were on the prowl, and that it behoved all those who shifted contraband from place to place to be cautious.

Sam crouched in the shelter of the hedge, listening to the thud of the flying hoofs and the crack of the long whip. The lights were upon him, and a wave of thin wet mud splashed along the other side of the hedgerow, spattering his face as he held the wet twigs apart. But Sam cared not a jot for this, as he heard the sharp rap of the billet of wood falling behind him on to the cobble path.

"There's a pretty rogue lives in that place," growled the General, peering through the rain-running window of the coach, and pointing to the deep shadow of the wide-spread roof, which could harbour hundreds of kegs in its hidden apple-rooms.

"Slippery Sam's, sir?" laughed Major Faunce.

"A very godless title," remarked the Archbishop.

"I'm afraid I always laugh at it," replied the Major. "The way he gained it was at least original."

"How did he gain it, and who is he?" asked the Archbishop.

"Slippery Sam, Your Grace," explained the General, "is a squint-eyed rascal believed to be in league with the Romney Marsh smugglers under that damned Scarecrow." The General coughed a quick apology, and added, "I should not use such a strong expression before so distinguished a churchman. I beg your Grace's pardon." The Archbishop waved his hand in acceptance, saying: "The word 'damn' is a good one when it is not abused, for of a surety any citizen who works against His Majesty's Government will in the latter day be damned and confounded. But you were about to tell me something of this Slippery Sam, Major Faunce."

"An unutterable rogue, Your Grace," went on the Major, "who makes out that his prosperity comes from farming, although the Customs men think otherwise. The difficulty is to prove it, and there the authorities have so far fallen down. Once they actually issued a warrant of search, and the Excise men broke through the back door in the dead of night. They made their way upstairs and thundered on the bolted bedroom door, only to be told by the screaming wife that her husband was from home on business. Not believing this, the officer in charge ordered the door to be forced.

"While engaged in the noisy and tedious operation of breaking through Sam's stout oak defence, the rascal smeared his naked body with oil and suddenly threw open the door and leapt out upon them. They grabbed for him in the dark, but hampered as they were by the steep narrow stairs, they might as well have tried to hold an eel. Sam slipped through them, took to the woods, an in the morning returned in borrowed clothes and driving his own trap, which he had lent to a neighbour.

"The wife had had ample time to see that all the kegs were hidden, and at the inquiry, which Sam insisted on taking place before a magistrate, there were plenty of witnesses who took their oath that Sam had been with them the night of the raid and had slept in a house by Ashford Market. So nothing was gained by Sam's nickname of 'Slippery'."

"And the house had been called Slippery Sam's ever since," completed the colonel.

"And truly has it been written," said the Archbishop, "that the ways of the ungodly are full of deceit." In the meantime the subject of this conversation had run his fingers down the notches cut in the piece of wood, and returning to the darkened kitchen had interpreted their meaning to the waiting men.

"The next 'run', lads, is for Thursday. The Scarecrow expects from us fifty pack ponies and twenty mounted men. The warning notch is again cut at the base here, and as you know, it means no firearms to be carried, but flashers for * signalling. In case of a brush with the Excise men, you can use 'bats'." ** "I don't hold with that," replied a rough young fellow of the company. "If the Excise men carry firearms, why not us? Are we rabbits to be potted at?"

"If an Excise man kills one of us gentlemen," replied Sam, "it ain't brought in as murder. But if one of us gentlemen shoots an Excise man, it be murder, and murder most foul, and that means Mister Ketch removing your neckcloth for a bit of hemp, see? No, my lad, we're all for the making of money and for having a bit of fun as well. I take it, and if so be as we obeys the Scarecrow in

*"Flashers" were flint-locked and powder-panned pistols without barrels, used either for signalling or tinder-boxes.

**"Bats" were stout hop-poles used as lances by mounted

smugglers.

Every way, he'll look after us as he always has done in the past. Take it from an older man that the Scarecrow knows the game and how to play it. So long as we obeys, we'll be rich men and never dance to the hangman's tune with our toes in the air." The company growling an assent, the young man kept silent.

When Slippery Sam had duly arranged with each man the apportioning of the ponies and horses required, he was called upon to answer yet another criticism of the Scarecrow's methods. This time the critic was an elderly villager from Sturry, whose outward profession was that of a thatcher, but, like Sam's farming, the store of guineas hidden beneath a floor-board of his bedroom had not been earned through his attention to roofs. He was an old hand at the smuggling game, and had been "out" as he said long before the Scarecrow had been heard of, for both his father and grandfather had initiated him into the business. Consequently his opinion was taken seriously by the others.

"What I says against the Scarecrow is this," he grumbled. "Why don't the fellow put more trust in us? There's only a few of our gang who have seen him, us being concerned with the 'hides' more than the landings and runnings. Aye, it's only you, Sam, Joe and myself what have spoke to him, that time he warned us that if we didn't get the goods to hiding before dawn there'd be trouble for us. And not one of us knows who or what he is, except a hideous scarecrow on a black horse. What's to prevent him from being a bit more friendly like, I says?"

"What's to prevent him?" cried Sam scornfully. "I'll tell you just that, old man. Just the love of his own neck, and that's good reason enough. You'll own we've never earned so much money at the smuggling since that little rat of a Dymchurch sexton come along with the Scarecrow's proposition. That there Mipps may know who he is, I don't doubt, but who else? Why, several of the lads down yonder on the Marshes have told me that not even the head gang, the Dymchurch Night-riders, know who or what he is, and so long as no one don't know—why, no one can't go turning King's Evidence against him, see? "He's clever, he is, and whoever he is, good luck to him and may he continue to keep his own neck along of ours from the rope. Who but him would have thought of using the blessed Archbishop's coach, as he did just now, to pass us orders? Who but him could have squared every guard on the mail coaches without being found out? Do you ever stop to think how many are working under him? It ain't only our little lot here he has dealings with.

There's the boys below on the luggers, and they'll tell you that he knows more about winds, tides, and weather than they do themselves.

"Then there's the Frenchies, t'other side of the Channel, to be reckoned with, and Hollanders, too, and they do say that he can talk to 'em and swear at 'em too in their own cursed lingo. Aye, he's a man of parts is the Scarecrow, so we don't let none of us start argyfying against him, same as them dirty Bonnington gang are doing. For my own part I'm just awaiting to see what will happen to them poor field mice.

"The Scarecrow will play diddle with them, as he does with the Excise men, and so I told them Ransley boys when they come down here and wanted us to join their damned cracky scheme of getting to work on our own, same as our grandads did before us. If some of 'em had been half as clever as our Scarecrow in them days they bodies wouldn't now be rotting out in Botany Bay. But if so be that some of you wants to swing—why, then betray the Scarecrow if you can, and you'll find it will be the Scarecrow's men what will do your swinging for you and not the common hangman."

So impressed were they with Sam's spirited oration that the old thatcher replied meekly, "All right, Sam, I only just meant that I'd give a couple of guineas just by way of curiosity to know who the Scarecrow might be."

"A couple won't buy it," scoffed Sam. "Ain't the damn Government offered five hundred of the best ringing spades of his blessed Majesty Farmer George just for the same bit of news, which they won't never get?"

"Aye," nodded the thatcher. "But that's different, Sam. They didn't do it out of no curiosity, but out of downright cursed venom." And since this remark seemed to re-establish the thatcher's loyalty to the Scarecrow, the company drank whole-heartedly to his toast of "Down with the cursed Customs, and God bless King George."

Chapter 2. The Archbishop and the highwayman

At its southern extremity Stone Street curves round the top of a deep valley, and then plunges down a steep incline, which is so overtopped with great and ancient trees that even in sunlight it is dark and gloomy. At night, and especially on such a November night of storm, it looked like an impenetrable tunnel of blackness, as the horses of the Archbishop's coach were pulled up in order to allow the guard to climb from his lofty box and adjust the skids. Knowing his team to be well behaved, the coachman, partly to save time and partly to take the opportunity of stretching his cramped legs, climbed down likewise, patted his steaming charges, and condescended to fix the fore skids.

At the request of the General, Major Faunce opened the door and asked whether the guard wished any of them to walk down the hill.

"No, sir," replied the guard. "I'll walk myself, while the coachman holds 'em back and takes it easy."

"I notice you ain't got your blunderbuss under your arm," said the coachman. "You'd best climb up and get it. You never know what's waiting for us under them trees down yonder."

"What are you frightened of?" asked the guard scornfully. "There ain't no smugglers out tonight."

"Just the weather for 'em," growled the coachman. "Besides, what do you know about it?"

"Everyone knows when there's a run on," retorted the guard. "That is, everyone what keeps his ears open. They was all abed at Slippery Sam's, and when there's a 'run' going forward they sits up and sings and shouts at their drinking. They've no fear of God or man, that lot."

"And who said 'smugglers'?" demanded the coachman, who by the light of an unhooked carriage lamp was examining the set of his harness. "Smugglers avoids one, I find, but I don't say the same for that there Jimmie Bone."

"Highwaymen works the Dover Road, not a cross-country cut like this," replied the guard. "Besides, I have it on good authority that Mr. Bone is lying low since his last hold-up."

"He'll get laid by the heels before long, same as they all does," grunted the coachman. "Well, I'll be getting up on the box again, 'cos I left my pistols up there, same as you did your bit of artillery. But there, a coachman has his horses to mind, and ain't supposed to be an armed escort, whereas a guard's a guard, and it's his duty to guard, so next time you descends, bring the old blunderbuss with you, if you please." Not relishing so long a delay at such a gloomy spot, the Archbishop querulously asked the General if he could see what his servants were doing.

"Anything wrong?" shouted the General, looking out.

The coachman jumped round nervously. "No, sir. Nothing's wrong."

"But there will be if you don't take your foot from the step," cried a deep gruff voice from the darkness ahead of them.

The coachman, who had been preparing to heave himself up on to his box, fell back on to the road. His worst fears were realized, as a masked rider on a tall black horse rode slowly from the trees into the glare of the coach lights.

"Jimmie Bone, by all that's damnable!" said the guard, and then turning on the coachman added, "This comes of you talking of the devil."

"What's the delay?" asked the General, once more thrusting his head out of the window. "Anything wrong now?"

"Plenty, my old gentleman," laughed Mr. Bone, riding closer. "To begin with, the weather's all wrong. As damned dirty a night as ever I rode in, so you'll oblige me greatly by forking out and stumping up as quick as possible so that I can take my long ride to safety."

"Who the devil are you, sir?" roared the General.

"Better known on the Dover Road than here, sir," replied the highwayman.

"You ask the guards of His Majesty's mails, and they'll tell you that Mr. Bone executes his business with what politeness he can, but prompt payments are essential, or he gets the very devil in him. I see by your coat that you're a military gentleman. Good. That means that you're used to giving orders and taking 'em as well. It also means that when you know you're beaten you surrender with good grace. Well, you can take it from me, sir, that you're beaten now, and better beaten than I hope you will ever be in the field of battle.

So just you pass the word of command along to your companions inside, whoever they may be, and turn 'em out one by one so that I can see the linings of your pockets. We'll start with you, my old soldier, so that you show 'em how to be smart and prompt." General Troubridge was too wise a man not to realize that his sabre was of no avail against two levelled horse-pistols in the hands of a desperate villain.

Also knowing the rules of war, he was not so foolish as to turn his head from the muzzles for the highwayman might well believe that there was trickery and shoot. So he contented himself with growling over his shoulder to his travelling companions, "It's no use, gentlemen, we're stung, and properly stung, and our only satisfaction is to know at least that this rascal will eventually come to his death."

"Alas, sir," sighed Jimmie Bone, "that indeed is a certainty to which we must all come, sooner or later, but as I do not wish mine to be immediate, I would request you to be prompt and step outside as quickly as you may.

Otherwise I may lose my temper. On a night like this one's temper is none of the best. Jump to it."

"It's outrageous," cried Major Faunce, as the General opened the coach door and descended the step.

"One at a time, please," rapped out the highwayman.

"Stay where you are, Major," snapped the General.

"Yes, for heaven's sake, gentleman, do what he wants," urged the Archbishop. "It's no use throwing away valuable lives."

"Now then, Mister Guard," went on the highwayman, "as each pocket is turned out, you will hand me the contents. Now then, Colonel, let's see the linings."

"General, sir. General," corrected old Troubridge, with a dignity that was somewhat impaired by the indignity of turning out his pockets, and handing the contents to the guard.

A gold watch, a fat purse of guineas, and a signet ring were the only items that attracted Mister Bone's interest. He had thrust one of his pistols into the holster as he took the articles one by one from the guard's hand and examined them by the light of the coach lamp. The purse and watch he dropped into the capacious side pocket of his riding coat, but the ring he gave back to the guard saying: "A family ring. I'll not rob a gentleman of his crest. Give it to the General, and I'll take your spurs, sir, instead. A pair of good spurs are always useful."

"Damn it, sir," retorted the General, "they are part of my uniform."

"Take 'em off," ordered the highwayman sharply, "or I'll have your sword, boots and breeches too."

Fuming with rage, the General sat himself down on the coach

step, removed his spurs and handed them over.

"Thank you, General," laughed Jimmie Bone. "And now inside with you and let us have a look at the property of the other officer." Major Faunce produced two purses, three rings, not signets, a gold watch, a jewelled snuff-box, and a diamond brooch from his cravat. He took his misfortune with philosophy until Jimmie Bone cast a favourable and inquisitive eye upon his sabretache.

"Full of military papers, no doubt," he said. "It will be amusing reading. It look bulky enough, and I dare say the loss of whatever documents it may hold will disorganize your command. Well, if it only keeps some poor devil of a trooper from trouble, my carrying them away will be justified. Hand over the sabretache, my officer. Next passenger, please."

With ill grace the Major stepped back into the coach to make way for His Grace of Canterbury.

At the sight of his victim's clerical garb, the highwayman uttered an oath, for which he quickly apologized with the explanation: "A parson, eh? And no doubt I shouldn't have sworn. But the sight of a parson in the way of business is always enough cause to make your humble servant annoyed, for I never yet robbed a parson upon the high-road. An old witch once told me that if I robbed a servant of the Lord my luck would be out. So you may get back into the coach, think a little better of Jimmie Bone, thank God for His uniform which has saved your scanty purse. Good night to you, Master Curate." The delighted Archbishop turned to climb back into the coach, when the guard sprang forward to help him with, "Mind the step, Your Grace."

"Grace?" repeated the highwayman. "Why, bless me, so it is, and I'm stung.

For if it ain't the old Aggerbagger himself. Yes, sir, I am acquainted with your nickname since I once kept company with a chambermaid in Canterbury Precincts, and she told me that boys of the King's School called you Aggerbagger behind your reverend back. Well, sir, I will not break my rule even for you, who no doubt carries more guineas in his pockets than your military companions." As soon as the door was closed against the Archbishop, Jimmie Bone addressed the guard with: "And now you will help the old coachman to unharness the horses, which you will hold on each side of the coach. This will keep you occupied and your itching fingers away from your artillery, for which service to me I will spare you the necessity of turning out your own pockets." The two servants quickly availed themselves of their chance, and as soon as the highwayman saw that the horses were being led to the sides of the coach, he gave them a cheery wave of his hand and, crying out, "My compliments, gentlemen," he turned his magnificent horse and galloped away into the blackness of the trees.

While the servants were reharnessing the horses, the Archbishop with a curious lack of tact remarked to the General that the fellow was not without his good points.

The irritated General replied hotly: "The fact that he did not rob Your Grace will not save him as far as I'm concerned. I shall hunt him down, sir, and attend his hanging with a great relish."

"I wonder, sir," said the Major, "whether he could by any chance be the other candidate for your gallows. I mean, could this rascal be the Scarecrow of Romney Marsh?"

"No, sir," retorted the General. "It's been proved very conclusively that they are not the same. Have you forgotten the occasion when this Bone held up the guinea coach and was in turn robbed by the Scarecrow and his men? It was the talk of the county."

"I remember well enough, sir," replied the Major. "But I have lately been wondering whether that many not have been a ruse, a friendly ruse on the part of the Scarecrow to clear the name of the highwayman. And yet why should the leader of the smugglers have wished to dispel a rumour so greatly to his own advantage, unless, as it occurred to me just now, they are one and the same?" The General shook his head violently. "My brother, the Admiral, was talking much the same sort of nonsense to me but the other day, and I don't hold with it. However, it makes very little difference now, for I swear that I will bring not only the Scarecrow but this highwayman to book before very long.

We'll see what our host has to say about it tonight. Sir Henry is a Justice of the Peace, and as Lord of Lympne he must for his own honour bestir himself and give us every assistance."

"And I am sure he will," said the Archbishop. "And so will the Squire of Dymchurch, Sir Antony Cobtree."

"I'm not so sanguine about that gentleman," put in the Major. "He is apt to get very testy when outside people interfere with his rule upon the Marsh. We have seen that in the past."

"Other people have to interfere," replied the General, "when he shows, or seems to show, no interest in putting a stop to the scandal of his Marsh.

However, I shall certainly consult him again."

"I think the wisest man to consult would be Doctor Syn, his Vicar," said the Major. "He is always out and about amongst his Marsh flock, and no doubt hears a great deal more confidences than the Squire. Whether he would betray such confidence for the good of his parish I cannot say."

"Doctor Syn is a conscientious man, certainly," answered the Archbishop.

"He is not the man to break a confidence that his cloth would forbid, but he might well see his way into persuading one of his flock to turn King's Evidence for the good of the community. I will speak to him myself on the subject."

"He certainly gave us very valuable assistance before," said the Major. "It was he who organized the Marshmen to assist our Dragoons, but the Scarecrow was one too many for them as for us."

"Ah, well," sighed the Archbishop, "as the Psalmist tells us, the ungodly may flourish for a time like the green bay tree, but eventually we seek him and his place can nowhere be found."

"Your text certainly fits this Scarecrow, but in the wrong way," remarked the General dryly. "I for one would be delighted if his place could be found. He is certainly the most elusive gentleman that ever I encountered. But I'll get him, aye, and this rascally Bone along of him."

The horses were ready once more. The coach lurched forward, and the Archbishop was again bumped this way and that as the stout General swayed against him with every jolt of the road.

Meanwhile, Jimmie Bone had descended Lympne Hill, and was galloping hard along the winding roads of Romney Marsh, till at last he saw the lighted cottage he was looking for, and which his good horse knew as well as he did. A lonely dilapidated cottage surrounded by fields that were broad dyked, and inhabited by an old witch named Mother Handaway.

The poor old harmless creature was avoided by the Marsh folk, especially after dark, for many rumours were afoot concerning her. Her cats, her cauldron and her eccentricities caused her to be shunned by God-fearing folk, who although smugglers were yet sufficiently righteous to fear the devil and his servants.

The isolation of the old woman suited our highwayman perfectly, especially as she owned a stable so cunningly hidden that the presence of his horse and another's was never dreamed of by the passers-by by day. This stable, built of stone below ground like a pit, was concealed behind a cow-house. Its roof was covered with growing grass. The door stood in the steep side of a deep dry dyke, and when shut looked like a stack of bulrush reeds put up for drying. It had been made years gone by for a smugglers' hide.

Uttering a curious whistle, Jimmie Bone leapt his horse from the road across a broad dyke and, crossing a field, leapt another and yet a third, which surrounded the little farmyard. At his signal Mother Handaway had lighted the lamp, and by the time the horseman entered the yard she had opened the secret door. At the far end of the subterranean stable the highwayman saw another black horse, higher, bigger-boned and fiercer than the fine animal which he rode. As he put his own horse into the stall, he jerked his head towards the far stall and addressed the witch: "So the Scarecrow does not ride tonight."

"The word has been passed for next Thursday," she replied. "A greater landing of contraband than has ever yet been attempted."

"Well, I didn't do so badly myself tonight," laughed the highwayman, sitting down upon a rough bench and emptying his coat pocket of the treasures.

"Two gallant officers, and a parson whom I didn't rob, you'll be pleased to hear, since you have warned me against it. However, the more I think of it, the more I regret it, for the old fellow was none else than the Archbishop himself, and no doubt rolling in guineas. Now then, Mother, since you cannot read and I can, give the horse a rub down while I glance through these papers which I removed from the officer's sword-hanger." Emptying the contents of the sabretache beside him on the bench, he went rapidly through them. "Routine work, Mother. Nothing but dispositions of troops, bills for fodder, lists and rubbish not worth the paper they are written on. Hallo, though, what's this?" Seizing one of the papers, he held it closer to the stable lantern. As the old witch watched him out of the corner of her cunning eye she saw that he was deeply moved by what he read, but she knew him well enough not to interrupt. She went on rubbing down the tired horse, and then saw to the food in the manger.

"Don't give him any more food, Mother," he cried out suddenly as he jumped to his feet, "for it ain't good for a beast to go all out on a full stomach, and it seems to me that I must saddle up again immediately." He glanced through the writing once more and then shook the paper in the old woman's face. "Here's as pretty a piece of military knavery as ever I heard of, and the Scarecrow must know of it at once. Store those trinkets there for me, though I'll carry the money with me. It's a mercy that I thought of collecting these papers, or the Scarecrow would have wakened up on Friday morning in Dover Castle with a sentry at his door and a gallows pole thrust through the window." Thrusting the paper into his coat pocket, and sweeping the purses after it, he motioned the old woman to collect the other trinkets while he once more saddled up his horse.

"Dover Castle for the Scarecrow," cackled the old witch. "And what of that? He'd be a match for 'em even there, dearie. He's the very devil he is, and the only chains he'll ever be fettered with are the chains of his own black conscience forged in hell. When first I had dealings with him, he told me he was the devil, and since then he has proved it a score of times. Still, good luck to him, for the devil looks after his own, as I have good cause to know." So once more Mr. Bone braved the wind, the rain and the darkness, setting his horse at a gallop across the Marsh to Dymchurch.

Chapter 3. Doctor Syn's black list

In the ordinary way of business, which in his case was robbery on the highroad, Mister Bone would not have imposed upon a tired horse which had already carried him many miles that night. No, the highwayman was too fond of his horse for that. Besides which, he knew that often he depended upon the animal's strength and loyalty. But this was a different matter. Jimmie Bone rode his tired horse hard, knowing that if he could not get immediate word with Doctor Syn, the pick of the Marshmen, amongst whom he counted many friends, would be food for the gallows. So on through the storm he rode, determined to reach Dymchurch Vicarage before the parson was abed.

Meanwhile, by the help of a roaring fire, a smoking bowl of hot rum punch, good Virginia tobacco, and stout shutters close fastened against the howling night, Doctor Syn and Sexton Mipps were managing pretty well to forget the storm that raged outside. Their conversation turned on cargoes, names of vessels and skippers, lists of "hides", carriers, horses and pack ponies, and every now and then the Doctor would rap out such a remark as: "Not sure, eh? Not quite sure. Oh, but we must be. Look it up, my good Mipps. Look it up.

Refer to the Register, the Parochial Register." Whereupon Mipps would drag from an iron chest a great tome marked "Register of Burials in the Parish of Dymchurch-under-the-Wall, County of Kent."

Needless to say, there were no burials recorded in that particular book, but only reckonings of contraband and other business connected with the smugglers. It was indeed the Night-riders' daybook.

The two men presented a marked contrast. Doctor Syn, as he rose to relight his churchwarden pipe from the candle flame, looked tall, gaunt and elegant, his long romantic face deeply lined, his cheeks hollow and his brow noble. A sad aloofness seemed to envelop him like a cloak as he stared down into the fire. The sexton was small and wiry, with an inquisitive nose like a sniffing terrier's, and had always shown such loyal appreciation of his master's greatness, whether as Parson, Pirate or Smuggler, that he had begun to be a comic counterpart of Doctor Syn. When they were together the sexton was subservient, though ready to amuse or to be amused as his master demanded.

But alone he would clothe himself in his hero's mannerisms, and hold his own accordingly with any man in the parish.

Suddenly the Vicar changed the subject of contraband by asking, "By the way, did you think of bringing me that coil of rope I asked you for?"

"Left it in the hall," nodded the sexton. "Nice bit of broken bell-rope, what I had kept as being likely to come in handy for the lowerin' of coffins. If you want it now, sir, I'll get it."

"Do," replied the Doctor.

When Mipps reappeared with vast coils over his shoulder, he found his master writing in a notebook he had never seen before. Too well trained to interrupt his old captain, he waited patiently till Doctor Syn had finished writing. Looking up, the Vicar caught the look of curiosity in the sexton's face, and as he closed the book he asked, "Wondering what this little volume is, my good Mipps?"

"I was just thinking I'd never seen it before, Vicar," replied Mipps evasively.

"Mark the cover, my little sexton," said Syn with a smile. "It is black. A black book. And the contents will be before long as black as the cover. Do you remember that we had such a book aboard the pirate ship, and that it contained the names of all the black sheep in the pirate flocks that flocked to the Spanish Main? Well, I find that such a book may prove of value to us here. The list is already started, and we must keep it in the iron chest yonder. It must never be seen by other eyes than our own. It will prove, as it were, a warning to ourselves, and a safeguard. And God help the name against which I put a black spot, for that will mean that if death does not come to the name in question, the name in question will bring death to us. In short, it is a list of suspected traitors and dangerous enemies, and it must be your duty to fix your gimlet eye on 'em.

Forewarned is forearmed, and if Death is to be let loose, let it not be our lives that are demanded. Aye, my hearty, this is the black book of Romney Marsh."

"Who's in it?" asked Mipps eagerly. "I'd just like to know, so as to adjust my spy-glass on 'em, so to speak, with no waste of time."

"You shall know all in good time," replied Syn. "At the moment, however, I happen to be more interested in the coil of rope, for if I can do with it what I imagine I can, it may prove a safeguard against one or many of the names that may eventually

be written in this black book. But I need your help." The Vicar took
the coil of rope from the sexton's shoulder.

"Get out your knife," he ordered, "and cut me a length that
will go twice round my body, with enough over to make a knot in
the small of my back." Mipps measured the required length
quickly, and then, producing a knife which he wore in a sheath
beneath his coat skirt, cut it.

"Now," went on the Vicar, "lash me up taut with a running
'Chink'."

"You mean one of them dodgy knots what the Chinese juggler
taught us in Malay?" asked Mipps.

"That's exactly what I mean," assented the Vicar.

"What's the idea, if I may ask?" said Mipps.

"Just an idea," chuckled Doctor Syn. "An idea that may prove
valuable one day. I marvel that I never thought of it before. I'd
better lie down so that you can get a good pull on it. It must be
convincingly tight, so you must not mind hurting my arms." He lay
himself down full length, face downwards, on the heartrug, while
the little sexton, with the skill of an old sailor, adjusted the rope
and pulled the curious knot taut with all his strength.

"You remember how to do it?" asked Syn.

"Try it," replied Mipps.

The parson strained with his pinioned arms till he drew in his
breath with a sharp hiss of pain. "That bites into one's flesh. But
I am grateful to John Chinaman all the same." He then rolled over
on to his back. "Now cut the coils in the centre of my chest,"
ordered the Vicar.

Still mystified, the sexton obeyed. Leaving the rope spread out
upon the heartrug, Doctor Syn got to his knees. "I shall want these
ends longer. I need a double turn around each wrist to hold it. Cut
some more lengths, and copy this design exactly but with longer
ends." Unknotting the ropes, Mipps did as he was told, and
fashioned the second set. "But what's it for?" he repeated.

"Observe," chuckled Syn. "I throw the knot over my back so.
I grip the ends beneath me, so. And when I lie down so upon my
face I am holding the loose ends beneath my body and at the same
time I am keeping them taut with my wrists. Now suppose you
were to find me lying like this and calling for help, what would you
do? What would anyone do who wanted to help me?"

"Untie the knot of course," nodded Mipps with a grin.

"Good," chuckled Syn. "Well now, don't you see that it might
be very useful to appear to be trussed up by villains?"

"Very convincing, sir, as you say," replied Mipps. "Likewise very tricky, doin' it yourself."

"Also, my good Mipps," went on the Vicar as he rose to his feet, relighted his churchwarden pipe and sat himself down in his high-backed Jacobean chair, "I have long realized that it takes the Scarecrow some minutes to transform himself into the Vicar of Dymchurch. So far this has not mattered much, for there has always been time and to spare. But, as we should both know from our own experiences, there are occasions when a man's life hangs on seconds rather than minutes, and therefore it is only logical that those precious minutes should be reduced to seconds. In future, therefore, the Scarecrow's rags will cover the Parson's cloth, and from now on, whenever the Scarecrow rides, he will carry this fantastic rope design sewn into the lining of his long wild cloak. That you will see to tomorrow." Suddenly Syn raised a finger of warning. "Listen," he said. "There's a horse on the gravel." Mipps heard it too, despite the noise of the storm, and then they both heard something else which caused Mipps to leap to his feet and pick up his old brass-barrelled blunderbuss which he had stood in the corner by the door.

Three hoots of an owl followed by the shrill cry of a curlew.

"The signal," whispered Mipps.

"On such a night as this the matter must be urgent indeed," replied the Vicar. "Whoever it may be must have sought you at your Coffin Shop, and then come on here. Use caution. Take him to the stable, and let me know, remembering, of course, that Doctor Syn had nothing to do with the smugglers."

Mipps tucked his blunderbuss under his arm, letting go the trigger spring which adjusted the bayonet dagger, and thus prepared to meet emergency he crossed the hall and undid the front door on the chain. Outside stood the rainsoaked figure of Jimmie Bone."Quick," urged the highwayman. "I must see the Vicar at once. My nag will wait, but my business cannot." The horse stood by the garden gate beneath the trees. "He is a good sentinel," said the highwayman. "He would let no one through that gate without giving me a warning neigh. I fear I am a wet visitor." Mipps led the way to the study.

Now Jimmie Bone had had good cause to trust the well-beloved Vicar of Dymchurch, so that on entering the room he did not hesitate to remove the badge of his profession, a black silk mask. The Vicar had also learnt long since that he could trust the highwayman, and so had not hesitated to allow him to share with

Mipps the secret of the Scarecrow's identity. Since they were both of a height, and both fearless horsemen, it was upon occasions very useful to have a second figure of the dread Scarecrow with which to draw a red herring across the track of hostile pursuers.

"My faith," cried Doctor Syn when he saw the wet coat and muddy boots of his visitor; "come in, man, and warm yourself inside and out, for to ride abroad on such a night indicates that your business is urgent. Dry your coat by the fire and take this glass of hot punch."

"I've no time but for the matter in hand, sir," objected the highwayman.

"Nonsense," cried the Vicar. "A gentleman adventurer can always find time for a good drink, and I protest that I will not listen to a word you say till you have consumed your first glass, and you may speak while I refill it." So Jimmie Bone swallowed the first glass at a draught, while the genial cleric waited with punch ladle to replenish it.

"My haste concerns both of us, sir," he said. "There is a piece of news which I have hit upon by good fortune which you must hear yourself, and for myself—well, when I tell you that within the hour I have held up another coach and taken toll of it, you will see that I have necessity for getting as speedily as possible back to old Mother Handaway's and safe hiding."

"Ah, you have take toll, have you?" repeated the parson. "Then I take it you have dutifully sought me out as your parson to whom you delight to pay legal tithe out of your illegal gains." This was not altogether a joke on Doctor Syn's part, though he appreciated the humour of the situation, because it was part of Mr. Bone's curious code of honour to pay to the parson a tenth of all his ill-gotten gains, and it was duly entered into Church Accounts as an anonymous gift to the Sick and Needy Fund.

"You shall certainly take your tithe, reverend sir," he answered. "Here are the purses, so that you can count it over yourself, and there will be more to come for your Poor Fund when I have turned some pretty trinkets into gold. It might have been a great deal more had not my conscience forbade me to rob a parson."

"Well, parsons are not rich men as a rule," laughed Syn.

"No, but I venture to think that the Archbishop would carry a few guineas with him as he travels."

"Have you held up the Archbishop's coach, you rogue?" asked the Vicar.

"But I did not rob him," replied the highwayman. "I contented myself with the two officers."

"What, my old friends General Troubridge and Major Faunce?" exclaimed Syn. "I heard they were accompanying His Grace to Lympne. Was this upon Stone Street, or nearer at hand?"

"To be exact, on Quarry Hill, at the very spot where you held me up after robbing the guinea runners. But, sir," continued Mr. Bone, "I think you have little cause to call the General and Major your friends, for they were hot on your track once."

"Aye, and will be again," laughed Syn. "Indeed, I have but a few minutes ago entered their August names in my Black Book, of which we were speaking just now, my good Mipps. I think that our valiant Dragoons will not let revenge rest though they are now promoted."

"I can soon give you proof that you are right there, sir," went on Bone. "It pleased me to rob the Major of his sabretache, which contained papers, and amongst them this," and he held out the document that had caused him to ride so fast through the storm. "Read it, reverend sir, and you will see that someone has betrayed the Scarecrow. The 'run' planned for Thursday is known to the authorities, and those damned Dragoons are counting on it to take the Scarecrow prisoner." Doctor Syn read the document through twice and then chuckled. "My dear fellow, although my cloth hardly permits me to applaud your mode of livelihood, I confess that you are a better friend to certain misguided folk on Romney Marsh than these eminent soldiers appear to be. If I remember rightly, this Scarecrow, whoever he may be" (and at this Mr. Bone and Mr. Mipps exchanged a wink and a smile), "distinctly scored over these military gentlemen last year. In fact I will go so far as to say that he made them both look damnably ridiculous." Doctor Syn continued: "This paper goes to prove, as you say, that their recent promotion has not cured them of a deplorable lust for revenge, and they are willing to use the might of England on their own authority to gain it. This will mean grave trouble to many of the Marshmen, and since these officers are no parishioners of mine, I think it my bounden duty to look first after my own flock and range myself against the officers. I will visit them and see if I cannot ascertain a little more than these details hint at. A full regiment of Dragoons moved from Canterbury to Dover Castle to be in readiness, eh? That shows a very serious antagonism on the part of the army against this Scarecrow."

"Whoever he may be," added Mipps facetiously.

"But you can find means to stop the Thursday 'run', I take it," said the highwayman.

"Oh, I do not think the Scarecrow would do that, do you?" replied the Doctor innocently. "No, but if you will return me these officers' trinkets, so that I can take them with these purses and papers to the General, I will not only see that you are compensated for your loss but will be told the exact plans they are about to take, and in all probability the name of their informer."

"If it is to serve the Scarecrow, whoever he may be," smiled the highwayman, "why, I'll return the full swag and be damned to the compensation. My night's adventure with all its wetness will be well worth my pains if the safety of certain people on the Marsh is assured."

"Thank you," nodded Syn. "Now have another drink and get away into hiding. Our friend Mipps here will call upon you for the trinkets and bring you the latest news."

"Aye, sir," replied Bone, "and I shall be glad to know what they intend to do about the robbery, for I take it that they'll raise a howl, whether the goods are returned or not." The highwayman's conjecture proved to be right, for the next evening, when the Archbishop occupied the Dymchurch pulpit, His Grace chose for his text "Render unto Cæsar", and thundered out disapproval against the local scandal of the Scarecrow and Mr. Bone. He urged strongly that it was the bounden duty of every law-abiding citizen to assist the authorities in bringing the rascals to justice, and practically accused the congregation of being in a position to do so.

Sir Henry Pembury, who accompanied the Archbishop with General Troubridge and Major Faunce, went even further, for during supper at the Court House he lost his temper and stated definitely that their host, Sir Antony Cobtree, if not an actual participant in the smuggling, was at least sympathetic, and no doubt increased his income by its success. Despite the presence of the Archbishop, and the calming influence of Doctor Syn, high words ensued, Sir Antony affirming stoutly that he was prepared to defend his honour in the usual way against any gentleman who doubted it. The Archbishop agreed with Doctor Syn that it ill behooved two Justices of the Peace to fight a duel, at which Sir Antony laughed, pointing out the impossibility of poor old Pembury fighting anyone till he had cured himself of the gout. This set Sir Henry into a further passion, so that he called for his coach, and drove back to Lympne Castle with his guests, in the highest dudgeon.

When Doctor Syn had calmed down the irate Squire of Dymchurch, he urged him to take an early opportunity of apologizing for the remark about the gout, when no doubt Sir Henry would also take back his unwarranted insinuations.

"I believe the old fool takes me for the Scarecrow himself," said Sir Antony.

"Well, at least I should take that as a great compliment," replied Syn with a smile. "You are still as good in the saddle, Tony, as ever you were, so at least you might qualify for the Scarecrow's horsemanship. I suppose you and this Bone rascal are the best riders in the county."

"Which is more than can be said for you," laughed Sir Antony. "Until you get an animal more fiery than your own, no one will suspect you of being the Scarecrow."

The Squire was thinking of Doctor Syn's fat white pony, but the Vicar, far from being offended, laughed too, thinking of the great fierce beast called Gehenna, which the Scarecrow rode, and which the Squire, for all his career in the hunting field, could never have managed.

Now, late at night, it was customary for Sexton Mipps to call at the Vicarage for orders, parochial or otherwise, and also to impart such news, parochial or otherwise, which he may have gleaned at either the Ship Inn or the City of London Tavern, for the tidings of the Marsh crept in many a mysterious way to these houses of resort.

On this Sunday night Syn's first demand was that Mipps should unlock the iron chest and give him the black book, into which he carefully wrote a name.

"Putting in another, sir?" asked the inquisitive Mipps.

"Aye," nodded Syn. "And no less a person than the Archbishop."

"He certainly attacked the smuggling, didn't he?" replied Mipps.

"He did," agreed the Vicar. "And do you know, I am not sure that he does not deserve a lesson. I should like to see him repeat that sermon, not in the safety of our church, but out on the Marsh one of these nights and to a full congregation of Demon Riders. It would be a humourous situation. Aye, very tempting. But there are other names to deal with first, and I think we shall be starting somehow with our old enemies, Troubridge and Faunce. The Dragoons are being moved to Dover tomorrow, in order to terrorize the Night-riders. Well I rather think that the Scarecrow may terrify the Dragoons first. We will ride to Dover Castle on Tuesday and open the campaign. Let us drink success to what I think may prove to be the Scarecrow's most daring adventure."

"Well, sir," replied the sexton, "I'm in the dark, certainly, but it has never been my way to refuse a drink."

Chapter 4. In Dover Castle

Two days later, Doctor Syn rose early, mounted his white pony, and accompanied by Mipps, mounted upon the churchyard donkey, was by noon being challenged by the Dover sentries. Owing to the fact that the cavalry had suddenly been billeted upon the infantry garrison at the Castle, a good deal of confusion and congestion was the result, and no one seemed to know where one authority ended and the other began.

Thus it was that Doctor Syn was kept a considerable time before permission was gained for him to enter the presence of the General, and in a mild way he complained of this treatment as he shook hands with old Troubridge. "I am a busy man, General, and I came at some inconvenience entirely out of service to you. In short, sir, I was very distressed to hear of your misfortune with that audacious highwayman, and was the more determined to do the little in my power to rectify your loss. In this I have been successful. I have recovered your property. Watches, purses and papers. It only needs for you to identify them." Saying which, Doctor Syn produced the various articles and spread them out before the delighted officer.

"But how did you accomplish this, in heaven's name?" he asked.

"Well, it was just that, you see. In heaven's name, and none else. I wrestled with the sinner's conscience in heaven's name, and so prevailed."

"You mean that you confronted this highwayman yourself?" asked the General.

The parson shook his head. "I could hardly do that, since I had no idea where to find him. But I did happen to know a woman of the Marsh with whom he has been keeping company. I visited her. I reasoned with her, and at last, on a sacred promise from me that I would not divulge her name, she confessed that this notorious and wicked highwayman had made her a gift of your property.

The woman I do not find it in my heart to blame. She has got into the company of wicked men."

"Well, we'll not ask you her name, since you gave your word not to betray her," said the General largely.

"But there is something else which I discovered," went on the parson, "and for that I gave no pledge of secrecy. Indeed my conscience rather tells me that I should tell you. On leaving this woman's sick-bed, I happened to overhear a conversation between some men below stairs who were not aware that I was in the house. In brief, sir, the robbing of your papers has informed the smugglers that you know the intended headquarters of the Scarecrow during the 'run' of contraband planned apparently for next Thursday. How you knew about this 'run' I do not ask. It is no business of mine."

"But I'll tell you. And very simple too," laughed the General. "I got in touch with a certain man whom I strongly suspect has been a smuggler himself. On the promise of a fifty-guinea purse with King's protection, he offered to betray this Scarecrow, which he did, telling me that his headquarters are to be at a spot called Walland's Barn."

"Ah," sighed the parson, "but you see that is all changed. The Scarecrow will now use a lonely house on the Hythe road called Cade's Farm. You could take him there. I can show you the exact spot upon the map. He will be there, I have heard, between two and three in the morning." The General beamed at the parson. "I am greatly indebted to you, sir."

"We shall be greatly indebted to you, sir, for ridding our Marshes of such a scoundrel," he replied.

"Ah, well," boasted the General, "I pay my debts, and I owe this rascal a revenge. As for this 'run' on Thursday, why, they may land every keg and barrel for aught I shall interfere. No, sir. Neither shot nor man will I spare on Customs business save to put a halter round the man's neck who dared to make a fool of me when I was Colonel of Dragoons."

"That would be my advice, sir," replied the parson. "Let the 'run' go forward uninterrupted, so that you can stop further smuggling by getting the Scarecrow."

"And by your help I'll do it, reverend sir; and once I have him here— But come with me, and I'll show you where I mean to house him till I hang him."

The General led Doctor Syn to the top of the Castle, and flinging open a door, showed him a large bare room with a great window devoid of any glass.

"This will be the Scarecrow's prison, sir," he said.

"Those iron bars are very wide," remarked the Doctor. "A thin man might well squeeze through them." The General laughed. "It would but save the hangman. Look for yourself." Doctor Syn climbed on to the window-sill and peered down through the bars. "What a height!" he shivered. "Never had a head for them. I sometimes get the vertigo in a lofty pulpit."

"It would be an unpleasant drop, certainly," said the officer. "Nasty cobblestones below. I shall post a sentry there, and one outside this door. He'll have the key, and will look in every half-hour, as there's no peep-hole, just to make sure the prisoner is safe."

Back in the General's quarters, the pompous soldier again thanked the doctor for his loyal services, and asked if there were anything he could do in return.

"Well, yes," hesitated Doctor Syn. "I should like to visit the Scarecrow immediately he is caught. I am somewhat successful in calling sinners to repentance. But really, General, even now I have no great faith that we shall catch him."

"Well, I have," returned the General, "and to prove it to you, here is your pass on my authority. Come when you please. Call the sinner to repentance if you are so minded, though for my own part I should let him go to hell." And so Doctor Syn left the Castle with a warrant from the General to visit the criminal known as the Scarecrow. And as Syn said to Mipps on the long ride home, "So sure is he of catching this Scarecrow that it seems a sin to disappoint him."

"Put such ideas out of your head, sir," urged Mipps.

"My good Mipps, it is time that the Scarecrow gained the reputation of being supernatural," said the Vicar. "I can see my way to make it appear so.

The time has come when we must strike terror into the hearts of our followers as well as of our enemies. I do not like the thought that there is a traitor in our midst." That night Doctor Syn once more closeted with Mipps, laid plans and gave orders, while the sexton, for the thousandth time in his life, marvelled at his master's supreme daring, which he grudgingly had to admit had never failed them.

His apprehensions were shared by every man upon the Marsh who had received orders to be "out" upon that Thursday night, especially when it became known the Dragoons had trotted in full strength through Hythe. But the grim Scarecrow on his fierce black horse, Gehenna, rode here and there, laughing at their fears and declaring that no regiment would attack his men.

However, this particular "run" was so vast, and so much

money per man was at stake, that, despite their great leader's assurance, a general nervousness prevailed, which did not cease till the last vessel had put back to sea empty, and the last pack pony had reached the hills to hide its goods. Then only did it seem possible that the Scarecrow was right.

"It would have been a serious loss had such a cargo as tonight's been captured," laughed the Scarecrow as he rode at a fast trot with Jimmie Bone beside him.

Presently he drew rein. "No nearer," he whispered. "I'll foot the rest.

Mustn't involve you or our good horses. Do you take my Gehenna back to stable."

"And if anything goes wrong with you," replied the highwayman, "why, I'll storm the Castle single-handed and release you or go hang for it."

The Scarecrow shook his head. "Things don't go wrong with me somehow.

So long as this gale continues, I am safe enough," and handing his reins to his companion, he strode off on foot towards the trap he knew was set for him.

Some two hours later Major Faunce entered the General's sleeping quarters.

"All's well, sir. Thanks to Doctor Syn, we've got him. He's safe in the corner Tower room. A repulsive-looking devil if ever there was one. Drunk and very ribald. Sang bawdy songs and uttered blasphemy the whole way. I tell you, sir, the whole regiment was half afraid of him."

"He'll be afraid of us in the morning," laughed the delighted General.

Chapter 5. The Scarecrow's leap

The night began to pale, though the land gale continued to howl round the Castle and out to the sea below. In the grey dawn Mipps entered the Main Guard gates behind a string of vegetable carts. But he did not follow them to the cook-house. He walked straight across to the Castle door, which was open. A cavalry sentry was talking to an infantry sentry in low tones. Mipps walked on by them bold as brass with a cheery "Here we are again." The cavalry man thought the infantryman knew him. The infantryman thought the same of the cavalryman. So Mipps passed unchallenged and was in the Castle.

It would have taken more than a sentry or two to keep him out. He knew the Castle well, and made straight for the Tower stairway. Up he went to the top and approached the wretched sentry, who had been shuddering at the prisoner's blasphemy.

"Who are you?" demanded the sentry with a start.

"Servant to the parson what has come to urge the prisoner to 'oly repentance. Doctor Syn, you know. He's down with the General. Look, here's the warrant for you to unlock the door. He'll be up here soon. My word, what awful language he's a-usin' in there!"

"Aye, what with that and the cold of these stone walls and the howling gale, it's the worst guard I ever mounted in my life." The sentry nodded at the signature of General Troubridge. It was all in order.

"Well, mate, for all I'm a parson's servant, I ain't narrerminded, and I have something here to keep out the cold. Halves, mate," and Mipps, drawing a bottle of brandy from his pocket and tilting half of the raw spirit down his own throat, passed it over to the sentry.

Nothing loth, the sentry gulped it down with thanks. "Good stuff. I could do with a cask of that," he said.

"Ain't got a cask on me, but I've another bottle," replied Mipps. "You have first go." The soldier had hardly taken his share when his eyes glazed and he staggered. Mipps caught him and lowered him gently to the ground.

"Aye, that was opium, that was," he chuckled. He bent over the knocked-out soldier and poured the rest through his teeth. He then drew out a third bottle, and poured good brandy all over the soldier's tunic. "Now you won't 'alf smell like an Abstainers' Outin'," he said. Then he tapped at the cell door and whispered, "Ready?"

"Ready," came the whispered answer.

Then there came such a piercing yell that it awakened the whole Castle.

Mipps fled down the stairs, shouting for Major Faunce. A sentry far below on the ramparts looked up to the Tower, and to his unspeakable horror he saw a black shape crawling through the bars. Then the Thing leaped outwards above his head. The gale caught It and blew out Its black garments, and then right over the Castle walls and out to sea whirled the wild rags of the Scarecrow.

With a scream of terror the sentry bolted for the Guard-room.

"What is it?" demanded the Major.

"What ain't it," retorted Mipps. "Oh, your drunken guard! Oh, your inebriated sentry! Oh, what a brute! You know me, sir. Mr. Mipps of Dymchurch. Oh, rescue my master. The Scarecrow's killin' him. Oh, poor Doctor Syn visitin' the prisoner on the General's orders too, and then that drunken rogue of a guard lockin' him in, because he was afraid to go in hisself.

And you should have heard the insults as he uttered to the man of God."

It seemed that the sexton was crying out the awful truth. The sentry was drunk. Not a doubt about that. He lay insensible with three empty bottles under him and he reeked of spirit. Also in one hand he clutched the warrant giving Doctor Syn access to the prisoner.

It was therefore with some apprehension that Major Faunce unlocked the door of the cell.

His worst fears were justified. There groaning on the floor lay Doctor Syn.

His neat clerical wig and neat parson's clothes looked pathetic as he lay there on his face, tied around with rope.

"Undo these cords. They're killing me," he moaned.

Major Faunce saw the great knot on his back, and kneeling down tried to unloose it, while the Doctor kept on struggling as though to free his arms and moaning.

"Let me try, sir," pleaded Mipps. "I was a sailor in His Majesty's Navy afore I took up with sextonin'. I knows knots." Between them they unravelled the cruel knot, and while Major Faunce raised the Doctor, Mipps secreted the ropes in his capacious pocket. He had no wish for the Major to examine those loose ends.

"But where's the prisoner?" demanded the General, who had been summoned by the noise.

"He couldn't have got through the door, because it was locked, sir," said the Major.

"I can tell you, I can tell you," gasped Doctor Syn pathetically. "The moment your sentry locked me in here—for he was afraid to come in himself—the prisoner attacked me, secured me with these ropes, which he ripped from the lining of his cloak, and then—O God, I can hardly believe what I saw—he wriggled through the bars there and leapt. Unless he is the devil, you will find him crushed on the cobblestones below." But instead of any report of a mangled body came the disquieting version of what the sentry had seen, namely a flying black figure with a great winged cloak that few far out to sea.

"Are all the sentries drunk?" roared the General.

But that sentry was more lucky than his fellow outside the cell, for other soldiers came forward, and Dover townsmen too, who swore that they had also seen the strange phenomenon of a black figure, arms, legs, and all, soaring out to sea.

The General, after venting his rage and disappointment upon the drunkard, whom he ordered into solitary confinement pending the rope's end on his recovery, at least showed some humanity towards Doctor Syn, who appeared to be suffering from shock, mental and physical.

"Upon my soul, Faunce," he said, "but I am sorry for the parson. He gets our property back from that damned highwayman, he shows us how to catch the Scarecrow, he rides all the way to Dover the moment he hears of the arrest, and then gets woefully treated for his pains. But he don't bear me any grudge. He said so when I put him in my coach, and sent him back to Dymchurch. He's a good man. A kind, forgiving, charitable old fellow, and I like him." Mipps did not accompany his master in the coach, for, as he told the General, he had to take back the Vicar's pony and his own donkey which had carried them to Dover. The presence of these beasts, which Mipps had seen to, confirmed the truth of their story. But Mipps made the most of the journey, for on a lonely strip of beach beyond Sandgate he retrieved the Scarecrow's clothes that floated in with the tide. While congratulating himself that they had all come ashore together, he noticed that they were roughly stitched together by pack-thread.

"Well, he's a marvel," he said. "Thinks of everything. Fancy threadin' a needle and sewing with all that danger round him. No wonder it looked like a man, and it's an ill gale that blows no one no good as they say." When he reached Dymchurch, the Vicar was reported ill in bed, but Mipps was allowed to see him. The sexton closed the bedroom door, tiptoed to the four-poster and solemnly winked at the night-capped Vicar.

"I hear you have been to Dover, my good Mipps," said Doctor Syn. "Very historic place, too. Fine old Castle, I believe. They tell me there's a window high up in the Tower there called 'The Scarecrow's Leap'. Nice things, legends, I like 'em. And while I think of it, find out that sentry's name. We owe him compensation. A bag of guineas with the Scarecrow's compliments, I think."

"Yessir. Any more orders, Vicar?"

"Yes. Brandy." And Doctor Syn fell to chuckling.

Chapter 6. The Squire of Lympne's wager

The news of the Scarecrow's sensational escape from Dover Castle spread rapidly and reached London by way of the stage coach, where it quickly circulated through inns and taverns as well as becoming the chief topic of conversation in the coffee-houses and fashionable gaming clubs, and, as Doctor Syn had conjectured, there were many who attributed supernatural powers to the mysterious leader of the Romney Marsh smugglers.

Down in Dymchurch Mr. Mipps did all he could to encourage this way of thinking, for he agreed with his master that it was a good thing for the Scarecrow to strike terror into the hearts of friends and enemies.

Although Doctor Syn appeared to be considerably shaken by the rough treatment he had received at the Scarecrow's hands, he did not neglect his parochial work, but was out and about amongst his parishioners within two days of what he called his "great adventure". He chuckled with Mipps at the sympathetic inquiries he received from everyone, and his usual answer was that he had no great wish to be locked again in that cell in Dover Castle. But amidst all the excitement, he did not forget to see to it that Sir Antony Cobtree should take steps to make up his quarrel with Sir Henry Pembury, and he finally agreed that he would accompany his patron up to Lympne for this purpose.

"And should he remain insulting, Tony," he laughed, "remember to keep your temper."

"Very well," agreed Sir Antony, "we'll go up there tomorrow and I will promise to avoid a duel if possible." That night Doctor Syn entered the name of Sir Henry Pembury in his black book, and the next morning he thought on this with amusement as he sat in the ingle-seat of the great dining-hall of Lympne Castle and basked in the warmth of the pine logs.

After a cold ride across the Marsh such heat was pleasant. He knew that his sturdy fat white pony that had zigzagged its way along the dyke-bound roads and then climbed the hill till the sea-mist was far beneath them was now comfortably housed in one of the best stables in the county. He appreciated the fact that the glass at his elbow contained the best sherry in Kent, which was whetting his appetite for what he anticipated would be as good a dinner as any squire in England could give.

It did not disturb the genial Vicar in the least that his host was at the moment in a furious temper. It merely amused him. From the shelter of the great fireplace he watched him. Sir Henry Pembury, lord of the castle of Lympne, was actually challenging Sir Antony Cobtree to a duel. This did not disturb Doctor Syn at all, for he was well aware that the affair would end in smoke, because his own patron, the Squire of Dymchurch, was far too generous a man to take advantage of Sir Henry's ungovernable rage. Poor Sir Henry suffered from the gout. That was the truth of it, and gout was a respectable disease that any gentleman might well come to.

That they were both Justices of the Peace and that the argument was upon Law and Order only made the quarrel the more diverting to the Doctor of Divinity. He wished that the two old knights could only see themselves in a mirror to realize the absurdity of the whole business. Pembury was an old, fat, ponderous dandy. Cobtree was a hard-riding sportsman twenty years his junior, for Sir Henry was close on seventy. The only danger in the quarrel was that Sir Henry might get a bad gout attack, for he was striding up and down the hall in an endeavour to appear as young as Sir Antony.

"I am well aware, gentlemen, that I am the aggressor," he boomed out. "But I am well prepared to take the consequences, and, as I have said, if it is a fight you want, I am more than ready to meet you."

"My good Harry," laughed the Dymchurch Squire, "I really could not think of obliging you, and I marvel that one who is so excessively loyal to the Government should suggest the advisability of two magistrates killing each other. Get over your spleen, man, as soon as you can, so that Doctor Syn and myself may enjoy your society, for after such a damned damp ride we fully intend dining with you."

"What you are pleased to call my spleen, sir," retorted their host, "I regard as righteous indignation. Are the doings of last night to be repeated without any protest? Are my stables to be broken open and my cattle taken by your damned thieving Dymchurch smugglers whenever it suits their convenience?"

"Come, now, hardly 'thieving'," urged Sir Antony, "for I understand that your horses were all returned."

"In the filthiest condition and ridden to death," answered Sir Henry. "You can see for yourselves, for they are not yet groomed, as my stables cannot boast of a sober man or boy. The whole pack of 'em drunk, sir, on the brandy left there by your smugglers. Is that not cause for the spleen? What can you say to that, eh?" Doctor Syn sipped his sherry and smiled. "Since I am preaching in your church next Sunday, I could certainly read them a homily on the evils of strong drink."

"None of your clerical jokes with me, sir," snapped Sir Henry. "I'm serious, and I repeat what I have said before. This mysterious person they call the 'Scarecrow' may terrorize the Romney Marsh. No doubt you find it convenient to take no steps to check him. But he won't terrorize me. Since he has had the impertinence to borrow my horses, as you say he has often borrowed yours, I intend to catch him and hang him myself. If you can't rid the county of a scoundrel, I can."

"If you succeed, sir," said Doctor Syn quietly, "I do trust that you will hang him in Lympne rather than Dymchurch, for, as I am always pointing out to Sir Antony, our gibbet is unpleasantly near the Vicarage."

"I shall deal with him here, sir," scowled Sir Henry. "We should never get him convicted at the Dymchurch Court House, for your jurymen would be scared of being involved. The rascal would turn King's Evidence against the lot of them if he thought things were going against him."

"I believe you wrong him there, sir," replied Doctor Syn. "Though I naturally deplore the notoriety which the Scarecrow has given to my parish, I confess that I admire his ingenuity and daring. I think he would never turn King's Evidence, since he has never turned his back yet on a comrade. In every case where a man has been taken for offence against the Customs, he has rescued him. A saucy rascal, no doubt, but, we must own, a clever one."

"He has made the Government a laughing-stock, I'll allow," returned Sir Henry, "but if he makes me one, he's cleverer than I take him to be. The wits in London may laugh at Dymchurch authorities, the Sandgate Customs, and those darned Dragoons from Dover Castle, but they'll not laugh at Lympne."

"Best be careful then, sir," suggested Doctor Syn solemnly, "that the story of your drunken grooms goes no further."

"I'll stop them talking," growled the Lord of Lympne, picking up a heavy hunting-crop from the table. "I'll give them something else to chatter about.

Aye, and you precious Scarecrow too," and forgetting his good manners, he flung out of the hall, banging the great door behind him.

"Harry's a grand old bully when he's crossed," laughed Sir Antony, "and we'll pay him out by drinking the rest of the sherry. Come, fill up, Doctor."

"Shall we drink success to his enterprise?" asked the Doctor.

"For my part, I would rather drink to the Scarecrow," replied the Squire.

"Well, let's put it that we drink to the better man of the two, and may he win," said Doctor Syn, holding up his glass.

"And that will be the Scarecrow, you mark my words, for if either of them is to be made a laughing-stock, I think Sir Henry will earn the title." So both gentlemen drank to the "better man".

Fortunately for the grooms, their master's whirling hunting-crop ceased its activities on account of the arrival of two riders leading their horses to the stables when the punishment was being carried out. One was his youngest daughter Kate, a pretty girl of nineteen, and the other a Cornet of Dragoons named Brackenbury. Though the young man came of good family, Sir Henry did not approve of a younger son for his daughter, and it added fuel to his rage when the soldier explained that he had come to dinner on the invitation of Lady Pembury, who it appeared had more sympathy with his love affair than her lord and master. Sir Henry was in no mood to hide his irritation, so it fell to Miss Kate to put her lover more at ease.

"Come, Mister Brackenbury," she laughed, "the boys will look to our horses, and dispose of your great helmet."

"He can manage for himself without your fussing," said Sir Henry. "You get along and change your clothes, and see that they lay extra places. We have Cobtree here from Dymchurch with his Vicar, Doctor Syn." With an encouraging smile for her lover Kate went about her duties, while Sir Henry with an ill grace gave orders for the officer's horse to be stalled. On the way back to the Castle young Brackenbury took occasion once more to plead his cause, urging that he had every reason to believe that Miss Kate liked him, and that Lady Pembury had already treated him with good favour. To Sir Henry's snorts at this, he attempted to paint such expectations as he possessed in the most glowing colours, but Sir Henry was not encouraging.

"I fail to see why a Pembury of Lympne should marry his daughter to nothing but expectations. Realize them first, sir, and then let me hear a more definite proposal, though 'tis most like it will be too late, as my daughter is of a marriageable age. But marry her to poverty I will not, sir." So it was a somewhat woebegone

Dragoon that left his helmet in the outer hall and followed his host to the dining-chamber, where he was formally introduced to the Dymchurch gentlemen.

During dinner Doctor Syn summed up how the land lay between Kate and the young soldier, especially as Sir Henry, outwardly using the Scarecrow for his subject, railed against the crime of impertinence.

Sir Antony, who had a great liking for Kate, who had confided the state of her feelings to his own daughters, determined to take up cudgels with Sir Henry on behalf of the lovers. So as soon as the ladies had retired he asked outright when Sir Henry was going to announce the joyful news of Kate's betrothal.

"And to whom, sir?" asked their host, amazed. "I have not heard any rumour of such happiness. Your own son is a bit young for my daughters, I fancy."

"I was rather thinking of young Brackenbury here," explained Sir Antony.

"You may recollect that both Doctor Syn and myself were at Oxford with the boy's father, Sir Robert, and I naturally favour the match." The silence that followed this bluff statement was embarrassing. Sir Henry stared at the young officer as though he had never seen him before in his life.

Then, as though his thoughts were wrenched unwillingly through his clenched teeth, he raped out, "Well, I confess that I have not been in favour of this match, but by God—" and he brought his fist crashing down on to the table as he said it, "Yes, by God, I'll give Mister Brackenbury a chance. The day you bring this infamous Scarecrow into this room, bound, and hand him over to me as my prisoner, you shall marry my daughter out of hand if she is free.

"These gentlemen from Dymchurch are my witnesses, and will tell you that whatever my faults, my word is my bond, and is never broken. If, however, the rascal makes a fool of you, as he has already made a laughing-stock of Major Faunce, an excellent officer as you know, and General Troubridge after him— well, then you must discontinue your attentions to my daughter. I'll allow you one month from today. If you fail, as you most certainly will—why, then will be the time for me to tackle the rascal myself, and he will not make a laughingstock of me." Thus was the bargain struck before witnesses, who felt no more confidence in the young man's chance of success than he did himself as he rode slowly back to his quarters in Dover Castle.

That night in the fastness of the Vicarage, behind closed doors and shutters, Doctor Syn entertained his parochial factotum, Mister Mipps, to a plentiful allowance of excellent French brandy upon which no duty had been paid.

"I find, my good Mipps," said the Vicar genially, "that as one gets older one develops a very tolerant sympathy towards the young."

"One does," agreed Mipps, remembering his pirate days and a young negress in Savannah with whom he had made a success.

"I look at you, my old Master Carpenter," continued the Vicar, "always remembering the days when you and I stood back to back and saved each other from a thousand deaths. In smoke and steel we stuck together on the poop deck then, and I am grateful."

"Referrin' to the days when we carried the gospel amongst the pirates, eh, Vicar?" asked Mipps with a knowing wink.

"That's so, Master Sexton," nodded the Vicar, "and we did well together because we each stood by, proving each other many times worthy of the name of friend."

"That's right, Captain—I should say Vicar," corrected Mipps.

"And now when I look at you I realize you're getting old," went on the Vicar. "Why, Mipps, your nose gets more pointed every day, your skin's cracked parchment and your tarred queue at the back of your half-bald head sticks out for all the world like a jigger-gaff. Your beady eyes are bright, though, still. You were always a shrunken little dog."

"My mother told me I was like a ferret the first hour I was born," replied the sexton.

"You've been fierce enough in a tight corner as long as I have known you," agreed the Vicar. "Your mother's description was right. And am I getting older?"

"Much about the same still, Captain," replied the little sexton. "You always give me the impression of a saintly archangel what can move and think devilish quick when occasion calls."

"Ah, yes," sighed the Vicar. "We retain a good deal of our younger days, I'll allow, and with luck we'll go adventuring till Davy Jones. But there are others, Mipps. Youngsters, nice children with good looks, but not endowed with our quick brains. We must do what we can to see that they inherit their own world."

"What are you drivin' at, Vicar?" asked the sexton suddenly.

"Merely that I am old and foolish enough to sympathize with young lovers," and Doctor Syn thereupon recounted the plight of Cornet Brackenbury and what had occurred at Lympne Castle.

At the end of the narrative Mipps shook his head, then winked. "Well, he'll never capture the Scarecrow, that's a certainty."

Doctor Syn refilled the sexton's glass and then his own, before replying solemnly: "You've stood by me in tighter corners. That young man is going to take the Scarecrow as a prisoner to Sir Henry at Lympne Castle, see? Unlock he iron chest and get me the dispositions of our next 'run'. Let me see, next Thursday, isn't it?" For the next two hours Doctor Syn and Sexton Mipps pored over detailed lists, checking cargoes, names of boats, concealments aboard, hides ashore, lists of carriers, commandeered stables, guards and signallers. When this was completed the Doctor ordered Mipps to leave him, as he had many plans to work out in order that the young Cornet of Dragoons might win his bride.

"So you've made up your mind to let yourself be captured?" asked Mipps anxiously.

"A captured man can always get away. I once escaped death on the scaffold steps, remember. We must help these young people. You are not losing your nerve, I hope?"

"Not so long as you don't lose your head," replied the sexton.

Chapter 7. The man on the black horse

The next day Doctor Syn rode to Dover Castle with a requisition signed by Sir Antony Cobtree, head Magistrate of the Romney Marsh Level, for an officer and ten troopers to assist against a possible outrage by smugglers believed to be attempted on the following Thursday. No senior officer wishing to meet with the like disaster that had befallen their General and Major Faunce so recently, it was simple enough for young Brackenbury, on a hint from the good Doctor, to get appointed to the command.

To the young officer Doctor Syn was convincing. "If you will pledge me your word of honour not to act on your own initiative but to obey me to the letter, I in my turn will promise that you shall carry the Scarecrow as a prisoner bound to Sir Henry. Such orders as I cannot give myself will reach you by the mouth of my sexton, Mister Mipps. But to no one else must you pay attention, or you will fail." The young man was prepared to promise anything to achieve such ends, but his curiosity made him add, "But how is it, sir, that you, a parson, can come by such information?"

"By reason of being a parson, and the friend of all, the shepherd of the black sheep as well as the white. You must not question me too closely, lest my conscience shall tell me I am wrong to thwart the black sheep in their sins. But I love your Kate and like you, and who knows perhaps this Scarecrow should be brought to trial."

"Of course he should, sir," agreed the officer. "You have surely no sympathy with such a law-breaker."

"The lost sheep must be tended by the parson," explained Doctor Syn. "And I shall do my utmost for the poor sinner when he is taken."

"What a very saintly man!" thought the Cornet. "If more persons were only like him!" On Thursday evening, on orders received from Doctor Syn through the medium of Mipps, young Brackenbury bivouacked horses and men beneath the cover of trees at the foot of Lympne Hill. In due course and under cover of the misty darkness arrived Mipps, driving a farm-cart full of bundles of old clothes, which he commanded the men to unpack. "You'll get the credit for this," he whispered to the young officer. "You see them other officers rode as Dragoons, and with shiny helmets and all. See 'em comin' for miles. Not you, see? Dress your men in these old rags like the Night-riders themselves, and no one's agoin' to question us." Leaving the horses tethered under the charge of a line-guard, Mipps crawled along under the cover of the dykes, followed by Cornet Brackenbury and his nine men dressed in ragged clothes and their faces blackened with gunpowder.

After a lengthy and zigzagging crawl the Cornet ventured to suggest that they were somewhat removed from their horses.

"Nearly there," whispered Mipps, who carried a blunderbuss. "Doctor's orders. He knows. Trust him." At last they halted, crouched and waited. There was no doubt but that there was great activity going forward. In the weird Marsh light spectral horsemen galloped. Gunpowder flashes kept on signalling. Weird cries were uttered and answered. "Keep still. Keep hid," enjoined Mipps. A cavalcade of ponies, some three hundred, passed, all carrying kegs. "Keep still. Keep hid," repeated Mipps. Weird witches mounted and carrying jack-o'-lanterns galloped around them. "Keep hid," repeated Mipps. Presently he whispered, "if you wants to see the Scarecrow, follow me, but leave your men here quiet till we wants 'em for the arrest." After traversing many dykes, Mipps halted, and invited the officer to peer over the top. "The Scarecrow," he whispered.

Brackenbury looked cautiously and saw in the centre of a dyke-bound field a tall, gaunt, weird figure dressed as a Scarecrow despatching and receiving messengers as weird-looking as himself. A great black unsaddled horse was tethered to a post behind him. "That's him," whispered Mipps. "Keep him covered with your pistol. I'll go back for your men; then as soon as he's alone we've got him." A few minutes later and the Scarecrow was alone, but Mipps and the nine troopers with blackened faces were alongside Brackenbury.

"Now," whispered Mipps.

Brackenbury was proud of his men. The Scarecrow, who leapt on to his horse, was captured before he could ride clear of them. He admitted his identity and asked where he was to be taken. On being told Lympne Castle, he swore under his mask and turning on Mipps said, "So it was you who betrayed me, was it, you dirty little body-snatcher?"

"It was," admitted Mipps, "through information received like. And don't you call me names, you awful malefactor." Piloted by Mipps they soon reached the trees where the horses were tethered, and after ten minutes' riding Brackenbury was thundering on the

Castle doors. Their arrival was most opportune, for the Lord of Lympne had been roused from his bed with the news that the smugglers had once more borrowed his horses, and that the stable-boy on guard was bound and gagged in the hay-loft. Sir Henry had roused the Castle in his rage, so that Lady Pembury and her daughters witnessed the triumphal entrance of the prisoner under Brackenbury, whom Miss Kate recognized despite his weird disguise, for they had not wasted time to get back into uniform.

"Gad, sir, I'm proud of you. Kiss him, Kate, and I applaud your choice," cried the delighted old man. "Now, son-in-law, leave your men here to guard him in the dungeons, and do you ride hot haste just as you are for Dymchurch and arouse the Squire. We'll unmask this rascal in his presence. Now, ladies, off to your beds. I'm the happiest man in Kent!" Off went the delighted Brackenbury in company with the horse-soldier, who was still in uniform, and up to bed went the ladies.

"And now, you scoundrel," snarled Sir Henry, "you shall taste the dungeons of Lympne Castle till the gallows is prepared."

"Oh, I think not," rasped the Scarecrow. "One cry and you are dead. I prefer you to be the laughing-stock to me."

Sir Henry was certainly not the happiest man in Kent next morning when nine unhorsed, disguised and disgruntled Dragoons, in company with a distracted Brackenbury and an amazed Sir Antony, found him in his brocaded dressing-gown lashed to the gibbet post of Dymchurch, with an inscription nailed above his head, "A laughing-stock, by order of the Scarecrow".

When Mipps was rated he protested: "Well, I did my best. How was I to know Dragoons from Scarecrow men when all was dressed alike? I tell you my life ain't worth a copper coin now from the Scarecrow's men. You see what comes of being loyal." It is to be feared that the summing-up of the situation by Doctor Syn did not please Sir Henry, for the genial Vicar only shook his head and said, "Well, there's no doubt but that young Brackenbury fulfilled his bargain and he can thank God that his father-in-law's word has ever been his bond."

Chapter 8. The sea lawyer

It wanted but a week to Christmas when Mrs. Waggetts, the widowed landlady of the Ship Inn at Dymchurch, sent a message to the Coffin Shop that there was a stranger in her bar, that she did not altogether like the look of him, and would Mr. Mipps be so obliging as to step along and cast his eye on him. Now any man not born and bred upon Romney Marsh was looked on as a foreigner and distrusted accordingly.

Obeying the summons, Mipps trotted into the bar and called for a noggin of rum against the cold. Casting his eye over the stranger, and thinking the weather was the most convenient tool with which to force open a conversation, he added: "And there's more snow to come, stranger. The old Frost Fiend ain't 'alf out to kill us this Yule. Dykes is all a-frozen, every man jack of 'em." The stranger looked at Mipps and gruffly replied, "Is that so?"

"It is," said the sexton, offended at such curtness. "I'm telling you, see? And my word's good enough on the Marsh, whatever yours is. Every man-jack dyke froze as had as your face. And since I'm a freeborn Marshman, and so has the right to the demand Who might you be? Lord Chief Justice? A Bow Street runner, or a French spy?—come now, speak sharp or you may find yourself in the Court House."

"I deny your right to question me," returned the stranger. "But since I am about to question you, I will go so far as to answer that my business in Dymchurch is of a legal quality."

The quizzical little sexton made a comical contrast to the tall stranger, who was powerfully built. His mahogany-tanned face and an anchor tattooed upon the back of his right hand showed Mipps that his antagonist was, or had been, a sailor.

"And you've followed the sea, eh? Same as myself. Royal Navy, me, though." This was true enough so far as it went, for although Mipps had spent the best years of his life as master carpenter aboard a pirate ship, he had signed on for a voyage home on a man-o'-war.

"Same here," replied the stranger. "But I don't follow the sea now. Always had a taste for the Law, I did."

"Sea lawyers I could never stomach," sneered Mipps.

"No sea lawyer about me," retorted the stranger. "Though it's true I'm down here on legal business, and if so be you could tell me where to find Hugh Brazlett, I'll be obliged.

"But first, since we've both served in the Navy—for I take it you're retired same as myself—why, then we'll drink together if you'll call for what you wish."

"Noggin of rum," said Mipps promptly. "Hugh Brazlett lives Burmarsh way.

It's a tricky farm to find, though, for a foreigner, but since I'm bound for Brazlett's myself, I'll pilot you there." With a curt nod of thanks the stranger drained his glass and buttoned his coat up to the chin. "Ready?" he asked. Mipps led the way.

"And what manner of man might this Brazlett be?" asked the stranger, as they ploughed along the Marsh roads, thick with snow.

"Prosperous farmer," lied Mipps, for although he had no great liking for Brazlett, he ranged himself upon the side of a fellow Marshman.

"Prosperous, eh?" repeated the stranger. "I should have thought otherwise." Mipps knew that the stranger thought right, for it was common gossip that Brazlett's farm had not done well of late years.

"Very pattern man, too," he went on. "Sings in the choir. A bit squeaky, but he makes a noise, and Doctor Syn is always in favour of taking the hymns noisy and hearty-like. Trouble with Brazlett's singing is it's apt to make the children giggle, and that means me gettin' out of my desk and proddin' 'em on the backs."

"What are you then? Parish work?"

"Aye," returned Mipps. "Likewise sexton and undertaker. And what might your name be, mate?"

"I have not asked you for yours," was the short reply.

"But you see, everyone knows me, and no one knows you. Fair doin's now."

"It is not necessary to give my name." And so in silence they came to Brazlett's farm, and saw the owner crossing the yard to his office door.

Now there was little to denote the farmer in Brazlett's face, which was weak and sickly. Mipps shared Doctor Syn's opinion of the man. "A worthy enough fellow. Pattern parishioner and all that, but I have no real liking for him."

"That's Brazlett," said Mipps, holding the gate open.

The stranger hurried forward, leaving the sexton to close it.

"Mr. Brazlett?" he asked.

"Aye, and you'll be Mr. Fragg. I have been expecting you these two days."

"There's others what has business with the London Customs besides yourself, Mr. Brazlett," returned the stranger quietly. "We've been on the track of 'receivers' for the last few days, hence my delay with you. But the King's currency don't depreciate in a couple of days, so don't worry, for I've brought it along." Now when Mipps had followed the sea, he had earned that rare reputation amongst sailors of being able to hear the hum of the old Quakeress's needle fifty miles out from Nantucket, which in plain terms meant that his hearing was acute. Indeed his ears were as sharp as his pointed nose, which seemed made to be poked into other people's business. What he had just overheard, moreover, seemed to him to be very much his business, and he felt it his bounden duty to get to the bottom of it, since the safety of Marshmen might hang on his quick action. Assuming, therefore, an attitude of complete innocence, and pretending not to have noticed the quick gesture of warning which Brazlett gave to Fragg, he accosted the farmer with, "Brought your friend along, you see."

"Thankee, Mr. Mipps," replied Brazlett awkwardly.

"And seein' as how he's come on legal business," went on the sexton, "and Burmarsh ain't famed for its scholars, maybe you'll find it convenient to have a man like me what can write his name as a witness, eh? If so, I'll stand by if you'll not tither but be quiddy."

"Tither? Quiddy?" repeated Mr. Fragg. "What the devil's he mean?"

"Ah, you be a foreigner," explained Mipps. "You don't know the true English as she's still spoke on Romney Marsh."

"Quiddy means brisk, Mr. Fragg," put in Brazlett.

"And don't tither means don't muck about, Mr. Fragg," added Mipps.

"Well, then, Mr. Mipps, if that's your name," said Fragg, "since my business with Mr. Brazlett requires neither witness nor signature, my advice to you is, don't tither but be quiddy with your own business and leave me to settle mine."

"All right," replied Mipps. "I've no wish to offer help where it ain't wanted.

My business is choir business, Brazlett. You know old Tom blew one of his silver keys clean off of his oboe last Sunday. Well, he did. The oboe's gone into Dover to the instrument-maker and won't be back in time for Morning Prayer, Sunday. So Doctor Syn's compliments, and he'd be obliged if you'll deputize for the old oboe by singin' a bit louder than usual. Good day, Brazlett. And good day to you, Mr. Fragg, if that's your name, and may the sea air do you good." Mipps walked away towards the gate, but stopped to stroke the farm-yard cat, watching at the same time to see Brazlett lead Fragg into his office.

Though glorying in the title "office", the little outhouse into which the two men disappeared was nothing more than a disused wash-house. A fire in the old copper kept it warm and an old Bible-box on a carpenter's bench served as desk. Since its door gave on to the farm-yard, Brazlett found it a convenient place in which to interview his farm hands.

Mipps knew the office well, and he now remembered to his advantage an unpleasant feature of it. In at one wall and out by the door there was grooved into the brick floor an open gutter, which in wet weather allowed a stream of water to run through into the yard. Useful enough when the place had been a laundry, but draughty and dank now that it was an office. Mipps had often advised Brazlett to block it up, saying, "You'll get the rats in after your papers." Fortunately Brazlett had been too busy to take his advice, and the gutter remained.

The moment he saw that the two men were safely inside with the door shut, Mipps crept silently to the back and, lying down in the snow, carefully cleared the drain-hole. He then found, to his delight, that not only could he hear every word that was being said, but that by lying close to the wall he could get a cramped view of Brazlett as he sat at his desk. Fragg was bending over him, reading from a long paper which Brazlett held.

"And you'll go to bail to all these names?" he asked.

"The whole fifty-seven of 'em," replied Brazlett. "I think I know more, but they might be what you call 'suspects', whereas these are in it up to the neck and all took part in the last great 'run'. The Scarecrow's a good leader, I'll allow, but he don't reckon the fact that many of his merry men will jump at the chance of saving their wretched necks by turning King's Evidence against him, and that even the Squire of Dymchurch will not be able to avoid a scandal.

Mind you, I still hold to my stipulation, not to be asked to appear in the witness-box." Fragg snorted: "But, man, under King's protection you're safe enough.

Besides, ain't you putting this farm up to sale? You'll want all the money you can get to start life fresh and safe in London. The Scarecrow's arm may reach far on Romney Marsh, but not in His Majesty's capital. You're too good a business man to refuse the extra five hundred guineas."

"Let's get this straight," replied Brazlett. "If I don't appear, I will get five hundred guineas from the Customs and another five hundred from General Troubridge if by my information the Scarecrow's gang is broken up. If it leads to the Scarecrow's arrest a further five hundred guineas from the same source."

"Remembering always," put in Fragg, "that it is the General's private money and in no way official. To think that a man is rich enough in this rotten world to lay out a thousand guineas to gratify a revenge!" Brazlett nodded. "And who pays the extra five hundred if I appear as Crown witness?"

"Customs," replied Fragg.

"It's big money. They pay well," hesitated Brazlett.

"They can afford to," replied Fragg. "Think of the revenue which these rascals are cheating them of. You take it. All you can get. Make up your mind to appear, and let me know. I'll lie tonight at the Ship Inn, and tomorrow go to Dover Castle with this list. I'm glad to note that your friend Mipps is involved."

"Involved!" echoed Brazlett. "He's the Scarecrow's lieutenant. I wish I knew who the Scarecrow was." Fragg laughed unpleasantly. "We don't exactly live in the days of the Spanish Inquisition, it's true, but for all that there are painful ways of making a man speak, and this Mipps will be persuaded to point out the Scarecrow. No use being squeamish when dealing with a rat like him." The listening Mipps that Doctor Syn would not be squeamish when dealing with these two conspirators.

After watching Fragg place a fat bundle of notes upon the desk, which Brazlett counted as his visitor put the incriminating list in his breast pocket, he left his hiding place and set off at top speed to inform Doctor Syn of all that he had heard and seen.

On reaching the cross-roads, however, he turned into a cottage yard and accosted a young man who was chopping wood.

"Look here, Tolling," he whispered. "You must knock off work for today.

Scarecrow's orders. Keep your young eyes skinned along the Burmarsh road.

You'll see a tall fellow in a great blue coat coming along from Brazlett's. When he passes, follow him, and don't let him out of your sight till I relieve you at the Ship Inn. Tell Mother Waggetts that your drinks is on me, and see that you take as much as won't interfere with your dooty."

"Aye, aye," replied Tolling. "And who is this man in the blue coat?"

"Customs," whispered Mipps. "And just by way of encouragement I'll tell you this. If that man gets out of Dymchurch with the list of names that he's got in his pocket, you, me, and fifty-five good men will be up at the next Assizes, see?"

"I'll watch him," replied Tolling grimly.

Chapter 9. By smugglers' justice

Doctor Syn listened gravely to the sexton's story and immediately ordered his white pony to be saddled.

"I must get the last proof against this Brazlett," he said. "When a man comes to die, one cannot be too careful, and when General Troubridge tells me that Brazlett is a traitor, then I will see that his death sentence is carried out."

"You say that you are playing a lone hand against these scoundrels in Dymchurch, and, reverend sir, I can well believe it. From the Squire to the sexton, the interest is on the side of the law-breakers. But take comfort, for if I have my will, the cream of your village will appear at the next Assizes to answer grievous charges of full proof. I know I may count on your co-operation.

You and Farmer Brazlett will be able to make a very good case for the Crown.

Frankly, I distrust your Squire."

"Brazlett?" echoed Doctor Syn in a tone of surprise.

"Aye, you can count on him," beamed the General. "He needs money, and we are prepared to pay it for information that will break this Scarecrow's tyranny. And by God, sir, we'll get him this time." After the loyallest protestations, Doctor Syn returned to Dymchurch, summoned the sexton, and laid plans accordingly, which included the ordering of twelve men, well trusted and as as strong in limb and as in purpose, to be hidden before midnight between the sea-wall and the great sluice-gate.

That night Mr. Fragg was enjoying his lonely supper in the Ship Inn common room when Tolling approached him. "Excuse me, sir," he said, "but Mr. Brazlett asked me to give you a secret message. If you will be beneath the sea-wall by the great sluice-gate at midnight he will show you the Scarecrow himself. You must not carry firearms, lest you are tempted to use them, for that, he says, would ruin all. I will be here before midnight to guide you to the spot, and let me add that I am with you and Brazlett in wishing to stamp out this scourge from the Marsh." Mrs. Waggetts saw Tolling leave the bar—"for home", he said. A few minuted later Mr. Fragg said that since his head was humming with so much drink, he would walk out into the night before turning in. He did not return.

Mrs. Waggetts, who had taken a dislike to him from his sharp treatment of her favourite Mipps, locked up the inn and went to bed. "He can knock all night for me," she said. "I'll not keep awake on the whim of a foreigner." Her sleep was not disturbed, for next morning the body of the "foreigner" was found in the mud-banks of the sluice, and it was perhaps significant that not a paper was found in his pockets. Mrs. Waggetts had to search his valise to discover his name and home address. It was obvious that an inquest upon a stranger did not materially depress the community of Dymchurch, since it occurred during the festive season of Christmas. Foreigners should not drink heavily and then attempt a midnight walk, not knowing the dangers of open sluices.

Doctor Syn had other matters to depress him. He took it very badly that Hugh Brazlett, "his pattern parishioner", and as he called him, was putting up his farm for sale and leaving for London. The good Vicar headed a testimonial for him and went from house to house persuading his flock that they must give good Brazlett a substantial purse and as a token of the affection and respect with which he was held.

"There is to be the annual junketing on New Year's Eve in the tithe barn," he said, "and the Squire has graciously consented to present Hugh Brazlett with our good thanks and wishes. Twenty-five years in the choir and altogether a devoted parishioner." The whole village were invited to the party at the Squire's expense. Mr. Mipps was fully occupied, what with knocking up Fragg's coffin at the charge of the Customs, and directing the decorations in the barn. Holly, bay and rosemary, and the jovial mistletoe in great profusion. And what a party it was that night! There was supper and dances, games and the Mummers' Masque performed on a temporary stage erected by Mr. Mipps for the occasion. This also served for the presentation, which was handled upon the stage by the Squire in a specially made purse. Sir Antony spoke charmingly of what Brazlett and Brazlett's ancestors had done for Dymchurch, while Doctor Syn, seconding, called him good and faithful servant and wished him in the name of the parish good luck in the new sphere of life to which he had been called. "The only thing we have to complain about," he added, "is the fact that he is leaving us, and yet perhaps when some of our young girls have done with him, his leaving will prove to be an impossibility." Here the good Vicar clapped his hands, upon which signal the fiddler, oboe and drum began to play, and from all corners of the stage there danced on a singing chorus of girls. Each girl untied her sash and bound the embarrassed Brazlett tightly to his chair, singing: "You shall not leave us. You cannot leave us. We have tied you to the parish with the sashes of our hearts." Poor Brazlett blushed at some of the things the girls whispered, but all was taken in good part until the diversion happened.

A great yule log was blazing on the open hearth to keep those folk warm who could not dance, and suddenly, and presumably done by some practical joker, a bucket of water was thrown down the chimney. With a mighty hiss of steam the log went out, and as the Vicar was sternly rebuking the jest and as in bad taste, a woman chanced to look up at the ceiling. She screamed and as she pointed, for she had seen two blackened hands and arms appear through a hole in the ceiling, feeling down towards the hook that held the tallow lights. Before the rest had a chance to follow her pointing fingers, these black fingers unhooked the light and dropped it, full weight, upon the floor beneath. The barn was in darkness. Women screamed and overturned the benches. Children cried and men swore. Above the uproar came the loud but calming voice of Doctor Syn, exhorting them not to panic, for he would find candles if everyone would only keep still.

Everyone obeyed. Nobody moved. The silence that ensued was only broken by some giggling girls, which Doctor Syn applauded and as a healthy sign. But these healthy sounds did not predominate, for almost immediately there arose in the darkness a scream not of this world, an unearthly sound that, arising in full strength, seemed to dwindle and gurgle down to hell. Again Doctor Syn's calming voice cried out that since many people disliked the dark, it was unfair of this joking screamer to add to their discomfort. "Whoever it was, it is a silly trick."

"A silly trick?" echoed a ghastly raucous voice in reply. "It is no trick, reverend fool. I put out the fire for a purpose. I let crash the lights for the same purpose. My name and fifty-seven good men's names were betrayed by that cowardly villain Brazlett whom you delight to humour. But it is I, the Scarecrow, who have seen that he has paid the penalty. Now, Doctor Syn, you may light your fresh candles and look upon Smugglers' Justice. Good-bye." At this there was a great screaming, pushing and trampling in the dark, but above it all arose still the brave calm voice of Doctor Syn calling for a tinderbox. After some considerable delay, which did not improve the hysterical tension, a light was procured, but on the first candle-flame that leapt from it, the panic broke out worse at the sight which met their terrified eyes.

Above the stage in mid air swung the sitting body of Hugh Brazlett. The four logs of the armchair to which he had been bound by the girls' sashes revolved slowly, suspended by the running noose that was round the dead man's neck. And as the growing candle-light increased against the horror of darkness, women and children—aye, and men too—cowered from the grisly sight, but too scared were they of the grim Scarecrow to venture outside the barn doors into the night.

The Scarecrow had done his work quickly and well. When the chaired body was cut down, life was extinct and the presentation purse had disappeared from his clutching fingers. When the roof was searched, they found, fixed to a beam, the pulley which had hoisted the victim to eternity, and a great hole in the plaster, hidden by a holly branch, through which the fatal rope had been dropped upon the chair. Another hole was found immediately above the hook from which had hung the chandelier.

That night, after the bells had tolled out the old year and welcomed in the next, Mipps closed the study door of the Vicarage and grinned and as Doctor Syn handed him a glass of brandy.

"It was a good thing, Vicar, you thought of that bucket of water for the fire.

Couldn't have done the murder in the firelight." Doctor Syn smiled and as he sipped his brandy. "It is always a good thing, my good Mipps, to think of everything in an emergency. Happy New Year."

Chapter 10. The bad men of Bonnington

Whatever may be said against the complex character of Doctor Syn, there is every evidence amongst the parochial archives of Dymchurch to prove that he was an exemplary country parson, always ready to give spiritual and material help to all or any of this scattered flock. His title "Dean of the Peculiars" gave him an authority over his neighbouring brother clerics, who found him ever a man of sound judgment, welcoming his advice on matters temporal and spiritual. His gaunt figure, astride his sturdy fat white pony, was familiar to every parish from Lympne to Lydd. Needless to say, these constant expeditions gave the Doctor every opportunity of listening to gossip of the countryside, which he turned to the advantage of his immediate flock.

Hence we find him one wintry afternoon reading the Scriptures in the sickroom of an old grandmother who lived with her son in a cottage at Bonnington.

To catch the fading light, he sat close to the casement, since the family were too poor to waste artificial light. As his rich mellow voice dwelt lovingly over the literary genius of Isaiah, he was aware that four horsemen drew rein at the cottage door beneath him. Round the side of the house came the owner, Shem Ransley, telling his visitors to step in and take a drink, as his sons were busy saddling horses.

Without hesitation or interruption of the glorious words he was reading, Doctor Syn overheard this conversation as well as noting the effect it had upon old Grandmother Ransley.

She shuddered. She closed her eyes, and the pain on her face was intense.

Doctor Syn finished the chapter, still listening to the conversation of the men below.

"Are you in pain, Mother?" he asked.

"In spiritual pain," she answered. "I can speak to you because you are a good man and will keep what I say in my old foolishness to yourself."

"That goes without saying. It is my duty," replied Doctor Syn.

"My son and my two grandsons down there," whispered the old woman, "have got the bad blood of my poor husband in their veins. It is not their fault.

The old man is in Van Diemen's Land. He always promised to escape and come back to us. Perhaps if he had, the horror of his transportation would have turned his blood from the same foolishness for which he suffered. He escaped the gallows only to go into exile." Doctor Syn nodded his sympathy.

"So sure was he of escape that he refused to take me with him, saying that a woman would make escape impossible." The old woman sighed. "Many years ago. I might have been with him all this time. He loved me, and he needed me more than the children below. They will not listen to my advice. They go their own way, and it is the way of the gallows." Doctor Syn crossed to the old lady and patted her hand. "Come now," he said reassuringly, "I don't think things are as bad as that. As you know, I move about a good deal and hear things said. People are good enough to trust me.

They do not trouble to put a curb upon their tongue because, you see, it is only I, Doctor Syn, and they trust the old parson as you do. I also hear many things from dying people, and the source of such tidings is never divulged."

"You mean you have heard something about my children to comfort me?" Doctor Syn nodded. "I know this. Your son and two grandsons refused to take part in the last smugglers' 'run'. They had been ordered out by the Scarecrow himself. They did not obey. Does not this look as though they repent the evil of their ways?"

"It is worse, far worse, sir," whispered the old woman. "Smuggling is in their blood. There is no repentance. But they are Bonnington men and are envious of the Marshmen down below the hills. They grumble that the Scarecrow pays Marshmen a higher rate than the men up here who work the 'hides'. I tell them that the Dymchurch lads run greater risks than they do. It is the 'landings' that are dangerous and the crossing of the Marsh. Fools. Why, the hills are safe, especially under the Scarecrow. But now they are determined to work against him."

"Against him?" repeated Doctor Syn innocently.

"They are changing the 'hides' without his knowledge," went on the old lady. "They intend to dispose of the tubs themselves and not give the Scarecrow payment. They think to get rich on one 'run'."

Doctor Syn shook his head sadly. "It looks as though it will come to blows.

Dear, dear. When thieves fall out amongst themselves it usually means bloodshed. Are you sure of this?"

"They are going tonight to make the new 'hides'. They have

collected men who are to meet them at the Walnut Tree Inn. Many men from as far away as Hawkhurst. The very name of Hawkhurst frightens me. I fear the same calamity as fell upon the old Hawkhurst gang when my husband was with them." Syn nodded. "I have heard about it. They were all hanged, but your husband."

"Thirty years ago," muttered the old woman, "and now like to be repeated, for my son will be no match for the Scarecrow." Now although Doctor Syn was genuinely happy to read the Scriptures to any old woman in need of comfort, it must be admitted in this case that he had journeyed to Bonnington on purpose to find out the very information which old Granny Ransley had so innocently told him. And so, having gained his object, he quietly and leisurely prepared to take his leave, though listening very carefully to the gentlemen in the parlour below, in case he could gather any further facts. After giving the old woman his blessing, he therefore walked down the narrow stairs and entered the parlour.

"Your mother seems very weak, Ransley," he said. "You must see that she is kept quiet and free from worry."

"I though you was gone," replied Ransley with an uneasy look of warning towards his companions. "You've been reading up there this hour, sir."

"She seemed to enjoy it," replied the parson.

"It's getting dark and you've a good seven mile to go, sir. Shall the boys bring your pony round?" Doctor Syn knew that Ransley was anxious to see the back of him. "Thank you," he said. "And what's that you are drinking? Brandy? Now after so much reading I could do with a taste of that myself." One of the strangers poured him a generous allowance into a glass, while the two grandsons, who were goodlooking lads, went out by the back door to bring round the parson's pony.

Meanwhile Doctor Syn chatted about the weather.

"You ain't captured the Scarecrow yet down on the Marshes I suppose, sir?" laughed the man who had poured out the brandy.

Doctor Syn shook his head. "I sometimes wonder if he is really human," he said. "I believe in devils just as I believe in angels, and I begin to think he must be a devil."

"Aye," growled Ransley, "if devil's luck means anything."

"But cheer up, reverend sir," went on the other, "for devil's luck don't hold for ever, and the Scarecrow, whether he be man or devil, will overreach himself soon."

"If only some of the scoundrels who work for him would betray him. But they all seem very faithful to him," said the parson. "For myself, being on the side of law and order, I naturally would be glad to see at least my own Dymchurch freed from such law-breaking."

"He'll be betrayed sooner than he thinks," returned the other.

Ransley coughed awkwardly, for the drink was making his companion too talkative, it seemed. Though perhaps the other men were too silent, sitting there in their mud-splashed clothes and saying nothing.

"I notice that you, Ransley," went on the lively one with a laugh, "do seem almost afraid to mention the very name of the Scarecrow."

"And that's true," replied Ransley, frowning. "You never know when he's going to spring up at you. The reverend gentleman's right. He's no man but a devil, and I pity any of those associated with him who might be foolish enough to betray him. Remember Brazlett of Burmarsh? We know how the Scarecrow punished him. Hanged him before the whole parish. I tell you, it's dangerous even to talk of the Scarecrow." Well aware that this conversation was but to put him off the scent, Doctor Syn changed the subject once more to the old woman upstairs, urging Ransley to call upon the Bonnington parson if his mother was short of nourishment.

"Oh, we shall do well enough for her," he replied. "I'm no great friend to our parson. He'll never call for a drink of brandy same as you, Doctor Syn, but, by God, we respect you the more for it." So in friendly fashion Doctor Syn rode away, conscious that one of the lads was sent after him to see whether he stayed in Bonnington village or took the long road down to Dymchurch.

Knowing that he was being spied upon, and having every intention of playing the spy himself, Doctor Syn put the pony to a jog-trot and did not pull rein till he had put the hills behind him and crossed the first great dyke of the Marsh. He then made a circuit to bring him back to the hills between Aldington and Lympne, and in less than an hour he had picketed his pony, well hidden in a wood while he went on afoot, and crawled into a clump of scrub-brush over the road, from which he could get a good view of anyone who passed along towards the Walnut Tree. He had not long to wait, nor did he have to strain his ear to catch the sound of Ransley's gang, for he heard them chorusing a ribald song long before they appeared out of the darkness. Besides this they carried lanterns, and he was able to count them as they rode by—some twenty of them.

By the time they reached the Walnut Tree they were acclaimed by a cheering, roystering gang of some sixty more. Doctor Syn followed them on foot till, hidden by the hedge facing the old inn, he was able to recognize many of the Scarecrow's men.

"We'll do our work first, lads, and then come back to drink," cried out Ransley.

Immediately they formed into procession and, followed by five great farm wagons stacked high with brushwood, they rode off at a walking pace till they disappeared over the hill. Doctor Syn tracked them at a safe distance, and watched them turn into a large copse, where they began to empty the brushwood in great piles along by the side of a deep ditch that had been cut for the purpose. Making a careful observation of the spot, the parson left them, found his pony and rode down across the Marsh to Dymchurch.The sexton, being summoned to the Vicarage on parochial business, found his master in a very serious mood.

"This is the greatest danger we have run yet, Mipps," he said, after telling all that he had heard and seen. "We cannot afford a mutiny amongst our associates, and I think it behooves the Scarecrow to teach these men a lesson they will never forget. Pass the brandy and let us work out ways and means."

As Mipps produced bottle and glasses, Doctor Syn unfolded a large map of the district, over which he pored, making nice calculations with a pair of silver dividers.

Mipps was sufficiently privileged to sip down two glasses of the good brandy before his master looked up. When he did, the sexton was relieved to see the tears of silent laughter in the Vicar's eyes.

"What's the joke, sir?" he asked.

"A very excellent one, my good Mipps," chuckled the parson. "Aye, and we'll play it too. I confess that at first I feared these mutineers more than all the soldiery in Kent. But inspiration always seems to come to one from somewhere.

A little concentration, and lo! one had found a cure for the worst trouble. Pass the brandy, and then I will instruct you in the part you must play in my next comedy. Perhaps you already guess the theme, eh?"

Mipps scratched his head. "I guess this much," he said. "We can't afford to lose next Tuesday's cargo, that's sure. You can see by the invoice from France how valuable it is. If these Bonnington brutes thieve us of so many tubs, we'll not only look silly, but their discontent against the Scarecrow will spread to our own Night-riders. I suppose you'll put off the 'run' till we can get others to do the work of the mutineers, eh?" Doctor Syn shook his head. "The 'run' goes forward. The twelve hundred tubs shall be landed as arranged. We must not embarrass our organization across the water."

"But we'll need at least two hundred of our best men to deal with the Bonnington lot," objected Mipps. "That leaves us three hundred men short. We must wait for new hands to come aboard, sir." Again Syn shook his head. "We shall only be short of the Ransley gang.

True, they must be dealt with, but why should we worry? Don't the Government provide us with an army of protection? Very well, I will see that the Dragoons look after our interests for us. Why not?"

"For God's sake, sir, explain," urged Mipps. "By your chuckling it seems that you've got one of your tricky schemes in your head."

"Which I will now put into yours." And for the next hour Doctor Syn told the sexton things that made the little fellow chuckle with his master.

Chapter 11. Doctor Syn's revenge

Two days later General Troubridge and Major Faunce of the Dragoons rode along the high-road towards the Walnut Tree Inn. It was already dusk, but light enough for them to discern Doctor Syn awaiting them on his white pony. He led them up the hill to the copse where the brushwood lay in readiness for the next night's "run".

"As my letter told you, General," whispered the parson, "here is most excellent cover for your whole regiment. I have ascertained that the men from Bonnington and Hawkhurst are detailed to wait on Aldington Knoll to receive the tubs. They will of necessity dismount here to hide the tubs in this ditch. The Scarecrow will be here to see that they cover the goods with this brushwood.

Your case against him will be much stronger if your arrest the lot of them while hiding the contraband. If you attacked them openly on the Knoll, they would abandon the tubs and scatter, while here you will have them at your mercy."

"And precious little mercy they will get too," replied the General. "Doctor Syn, your strategy is good. So good, in fact, that it seems a pity you were not a soldier yourself."

"But I am," replied Doctor Syn, solemnly removing his clerical hat and casting his eyes up to heaven.

"What a good man!" thought the General.

"I only hope that I shall not be held responsible for these wretches' deaths," went on the parson. "It is a dreadful thing to have man's blood upon one's conscience."

"You need not worry, sir," replied the General. "You are making a brave stroke on the side of right and justice."

"I pray that my conscience will continue to tell me so," replied Doctor Syn piously.

Tuesday night was dark, and the sea calm. The conditions for the landing were ideal. General Troubridge had taken precaution to warn the Sandgate Custom officers against preventing the landing.

Into Dymchurch Bay the smuggling fleet crept close to the beach, and under the direction of the tall Scarecrow upon his magnificent black horse the tubs were dragged ashore by willing hands. The first two hundred were carried by men on slings, two tubs to a man, and within a quarter of an hour from anchoring, this procession started for the hills, where they were glad enough to hand over their heavy burdens to the Ransley crowd, who accepted them some hundred strong.

Not a hint of these Bonnington men's treachery had been passed to the Dymchurch Night-riders. Doctor Syn and Mipps had seen to that. Having secured the remaining tubs upon the pack ponies, off trotted the wild cavalcade with shrieking witches guarding them and led by the Scarecrow himself.

Thinking that they would naturally follow the tub-carriers who had preceded them with the first lot to the hills, they were astonished at being led through Romney and Lydd out on to the wild shingled wastes of Dungeness. But they trusted their Scarecrow, and on being called to halt, they unslung the cargo into a deep dip of the shingle and covered it with a vast landslide of pebbles.

As the first streaks of dawn lit up the desolate peninsula not a sign of a tub could be seen upon the Ness, and on the Scarecrow's order to scatter in small parties for home, every man knew that the hiding-place was known to their leader and that in his own good time he would give orders to shift it into more commercial spots.

In the meantime Ransley, well pleased that his men had stolen the first two hundred tubs without a blow, had led his men to the new hiding-place, where disaster awaited them. When the Dragoons closed in on them and pushed them into the ditch upon the tubs, Ransley, seeing that the game was up, advised his followers to surrender without firing a shot, for by such a policy he hoped to save himself and them from the extreme penalty.

The next morning the news crept from inn to inn upon the Marsh that through their own treachery the Bonnington men were huddled together under lock and key in Sandgate Castle, in company with two hundred good tubs. The loss of the latter was taken philosophically by the successful Marshmen, since the gain on a thousand lying snug in Dungeness would be considerable.

When the tubs had been stored in a cellar of the Castle, General Troubridge kept the key himself and set a strong guard outside, fearing an attempt at rescue by the Scarecrow's men. He also took steps for an immediate trial in the Castle, to be presided over by the Warden of the Cinque Ports, thus preventing any local magistrates from showing indulgence.

The trial caused a great stir. When it became obvious that the Scarecrow himself had not been caught, the Crown pressed hard for the extreme penalty.

Both judge and jury were biased against the prisoners. Everyone, including the prisoners, guess the verdict would be death. The final case for the prosecution took place on a Saturday, and was such a long and venomous tirade that the court had to be adjourned till the Monday, when judgment would be given.

That Sunday, after Morning Prayer, Doctor Syn thought so sadly upon the state of old Grandmother Ransley that he saddled his pony and rode over to Bonnington. He found her prepared for the worst, but terribly distressed for her two young grandsons, who were, she said, "but yet upon the threshold of life", and she could hardly be comforted even though Doctor Syn promised to do what he could in the way of pleading for mercy.

When the Judge took his seat upon the Monday he picked up a sealed paper that lay upon his desk, and read, To be opened and read out by the Judge to the prisoners.

He broke the seal and read, "The Scarecrow's compliments to the learned Judge, and will he inform the prisoners that the Scarecrow has no intention to rescue them. Their treachery be upon their own heads." This caused a sensation, for no one could explain how the paper had come to be there. Doctor Syn, who had asked to be in court in order to read the wretched prisoners a homily upon repentance, asked to see the paper. He then produced another in the same handwriting, which he said he had found pushed beneath his Vicarage door that morning. It was as threatening, he said, and read out, "If the Reverend Doctor Syn attempts to rescue the prisoners in Sandgate he will fall foul of the Scarecrow."

"But how does the scoundrel think that you could rescue them, even if you wanted to?" asked the Judge.

"Because," replied Syn, "I have mentioned to one or two folk a theory, which if proved true would certainly save these men from the rigour of the law."

"What theory?" asked the Judge.

"Well, would this Scarecrow, knowing the prisoners' treachery, as he undoubtedly did—well, would he have wasted two hundred tubs of expensive spirits with which to bait his trap? I have not heard that the contents of the tubs have been examined. If they contain contraband, then no doubt the prisoners can be condemned; but knowing something of the greed of this Scarecrow, it seems to me doubtful. Ought not the tubs to be examined?"

The defending Counsel, who had undertaken the case with no hope for success, clutched at this straw, and insisted that what

Doctor Syn had said was only just. The consequence was that General Troubridge went himself to the cellar to investigate.

After some time he came back to the crowded court with a face of thunder.

"The tubs contain dirty water!" he ejaculated.

"And there is no law in England that can hang a man for carrying tubs of that," cried out the triumphant Counsel for defence.

And so it was found. Whereupon the prisoners, blessing the wisdom of Doctor Syn, were cautioned and acquitted.

"But what made you get the scoundrels off like that?" asked Mipps, when that night he and the Vicar discussed the matter together by the study fire.

"The thought of that old woman's distress as she lay praying on her bed at Bonnington," replied Doctor Syn with a smile. "Besides, Mipps, it seems to me a good thing for our safety that Doctor Syn, by the act he performed today, goes in fear of his life from the dreaded Scarecrow." Whereupon Mipps grinned.

Chapter 12. The French privateer

If pity be akin to love, then Doctor Syn, Vicar of Dymchurch, had a kindly feeling towards General Troubridge. The old soldier had been made a laughing-stock for having allowed the Scarecrow and his smugglers to slip through his fingers so many times, and no one delighted more in bringing up the joke against him than his twin brother, Admiral Troubridge, who was in command of Channel defence, flying his flag aboard the Vengeance in Dover harbour.

At last, however, the General found means to turn the tables and point back the finger of scorn at his brother, for a certain Captain Delacroix, commanding a French privateer, had for some months taken heavy toll of British shipping, and despite the most rigorous action on the part of the Admiralty, he yet remained successfully afloat. This fact enabled the General to reply to his brother's cruel lampoon of All the King's horses and all the King's men, Never will capture the Scarecrow agen, with All the King's sailors with cannon and ball Never will capture the Froggy at all.

Doctor Syn heard of this fraternal struggle and enjoyed the joke. Meanwhile the Frenchmen thrived in the Channel, just as the Scarecrow thrived on Romney Marsh.

Doctor Syn, meeting the brothers at dinner, jocularly suggested that the Admiral should employ the Scarecrow to catch the privateer, affirming that his mysterious and notorious parishioner, having never yet lost a smuggling lugger, must possess something of a nautical genius. "In fact, set a thief to catch a thief, my dear Admiral," he laughed.

"I'd like to catch the Scarecrow," the Admiral had replied, "just for the satisfaction of sending him in irons to my brother's Dragoons." And then came the news that Captain Delacroix had captured the contraband cargoes of two luggers trading for the Scarecrow.

"Ho, ho," chuckled Doctor Syn when he next met the Admiral. "If this news is true, then the Admiralty will have no more cause to worry you over such a water-rat as this Frenchman, for, believe me, the Scarecrow will never tolerate being robbed. There will be quick reprisal. The British thief will not be plundered by the French thief, you will see." And that very night Doctor Syn sat with Sexton Mipps in the Vicarage study at Dymchurch. The shutters were fastened. The doors were locked. The Vicar sat at his large old oak refectory table, upon which had been pinned a chart of the Channel. He also kept referring to a list of vessels which the sexton had produced from an iron chest. For a long time the Vicar made notes and calculations.

"The Greyhound is the boat for our purpose, Mipps," he said at last. "She's clipper built, fast and draws little enough water." The sexton shook his head. "She's only armed fore and aft," he objected, "two guns in all, while the Froggy carries fourteen, all heavier than them two toys on the Greyhound."

"If the Froggy (as you disrespectfully call him)," smiled Syn, "expects me to lay alongside, he's mighty mistaken, for I am not such a fool as to give him a broadside target. Neither do I intend to give Admiral Troubridge a chance of broadsiding the Frenchman with any of his seventy-fours. That would not be sportsmanlike. If we cannot run a fox down with the hounds, we do not shoot him, I trust."

"But what's old Troubridge got to do with it, sir?" asked the sexton.

"Oh, I'm just taking him along to see the fun," replied Syn. "You will be dressed as Hellspite, I as the Scarecrow, and a double crew as Night-riders.

And if I give the Vengeance men a lesson in navigation I shall expect you to give them one in gun-laying."

"Aye, that's talking," chuckled Mipps. "I always said in the old days that I should have stayed Master Gunner and not been elected Master Carpenter."

"You could lay a gun, I'll admit," said Syn. "And I am hoping that you will show these Royal Navy lads how to do it."

"But what'll happen?" asked Mipps doubtfully. "Supposin' that we get the best of this Frenchman—"

"Supposing?" asked Syn scornfully. "That rascal has robbed me of tubs. Can you doubt for a moment that I shall not get the best of him?"

"But remember what the Admiral told you," cautioned Mipps. "He said he'd send the Scarecrow in chains to that damned old Dragoon his brother. You're never going to get into the General's clutches again?"

"My good Mipps, our mutual friend the Scarecrow may run a particular risk once, but next time he is wise enough to ring the changes. Your General will not get me a second time walking into Dover Castle as a prisoner. Be easy. The only risk in this adventure is the fact that we are collecting the flagship to act as our escort, but against that risk I gamble that the Admiral will first wish to capture the Frenchman and the Scarecrow afterwards. Now then, give me some more brandy and we'll lay our plans."

A few days later, the Admiral, in response to Doctor Syn's request, was graciously pleased to show the learned cleric over his flagship. The Vicar greatly amused the Admiral with his innocent questions, his wonder, and his terror at having to climb rope ladders.

When all the mysteries of such a great ship of the line had been explained, Doctor Syn was led to the Admiral's cabin to partake of sherry before dining. It was while they were sipping their wine, and the parson was plying the Admiral with questions, that the old sea-dog picked up a paper from his chart-table. It was sealed, and on inquiry no one seemed to know who had placed it there.

Certainly the innocent parson with his naive questions on nautical matters was never suspected. He continued to blink through his spectacles at the wonders around him, till the Admiral broke the seal and roared out, "Of all the unparalleled pieces of impertinence!"

"Why, whatever—?" asked the parson.

"Your Romney Marsh scoundrel," roared on the Admiral. "Listen, I'll read it to you. Tomorrow night, whatever sea may be running, I will be lying off the fairway opposite the entrance of Dover harbour, with my bow down Channel. I will signal you with a flasher. Three long and two shorts, till you reply. If you wish me to do what apparently the King's Navy cannot do, you will follow my stern lantern, which will be orange, at two cables' length, and I, the Scarecrow, will show you that I can capture this impertinent Frenchman Delacroix. I will further hand him over to you and thank you to keep him prisoner so that he cannot rob me of any more of my cargoes of contraband.

Now, Doctor Syn, did you ever hear such bragging nonsense in your life?"

Doctor Syn blinked through his spectacles and then replied mildly.

"Bragging? Well, I don't know. This Scarecrow, whoever he may be, has a curious knack of keeping his word, and if he captures this Frenchman for you, I fail to see that you will have cause of complaint."

"Upon my soul," retorted the Admiral, "I believe I shall go."

"Of course you will," replied Doctor Syn. "I cannot imagine you missing such an adventure."

"You're right," replied the old sea-dog. "I will not miss it. And if you've the mind, why, tomorrow night I'll give you a berth aboard the Vengeance and you shall see the fun too." Doctor Syn shook his head. "And what should the old parson do in the midst of fighting men? No, sir, I am too fond of peace, aye, and of the land too."

Chapter 13. The Scarecrow keeps his word

The next day all shore leave was cancelled aboard the Vengeance. Guns and ammunition were looked to, and at dusk all hands were piped to action stations.

The moon was nearly at the full, so that as night set in the Channel was plainly visible. There was a good sea running, for the wind was strong, blowing great white clouds across the moon. It wanted but an hour to midnight when the lookout reported a vessel signalling from the fairway. The Admiral went on deck and made out a long slender vessel rigged fore and aft, that had come to anchor bow pointing down Channel.

"Well, I'm damned," ejaculated the Admiral. "That's her signal right enough. I never thought the rogue would keep his word." He thereupon ordered the captain to sail out of the harbour and to fetch up within two cables of the stranger's stern.

"She looks French by her cut, sir," said the Captain. "Suppose it's the privateer and not this Scarecrow. Do you think they are in league?"

"They'll get pepper together if they are," the Admiral replied, with his glass upon the vessel. "But I think not. However, they can hardly do us any harm." As they tacked round and approached the vessel they saw that the stern light was fashioned in the shape of a jack-o'-lantern. A mighty pumpkin, with an orange light behind the eyes and grinning mouth. The man-o'-war hailed her, asking what ship and flag.

For answer there was hoisted to the peak the flapping figure of a scarecrow.

"A good enough omen," laughed the Admiral. "For one day soon this Scarecrow will hang. And look, sure enough there is the very rascal by the tiller." With a mighty howling and shrieking which might have been derision or enthusiasm, some fifty figures arose from the deck and waved their arms over the bulwarks, while standing by the tiller the tallest, wildest figure of them all cried out in a raucous voice: "Greetings to the Vengeance and the great Admiral. If you're for seeing British beat the French, follow in our wake. We're off to recover the worth of our tubs from the French privateer." He sang out an order and his wild screaming Night-riders, now turned sailors, dashed to the ropes, and the

Greyhound's sails took the wind as the anchor was weighed, and she was skimming over the sea with the speed of her own name, followed by the slower-going man-o'-war.

The Scarecrow knew his course, for he had arranged that certain of his plans should be betrayed to Captain Delacroix from some of his own French associates, who hated the French captain for having robbed them. Behind them lumbered the great ship of the line. For four hours they sailed on a zigzag course down but steadily across the Channel. The Scarecrow took care that his great escort did not lose sight of him. He calculated that they must be within eight miles of the French coast when they heard cannon fire.

"That will be our decoy luring him towards us," said the Scarecrow to Hellspite.

"And that looks to me like 'em," replied the wildly dressed sexton.

Sure enough Mipps was right, and presently across their course flew two luggers with a larger one that carried more sail in pursuit. "That's Delacroix," said the Scarecrow. "Put a shot across her bows."

Mipps laid his gun and fired. A great splash arose within ten yards of the privateer's bows, but she held her course.

"Halve the distance, Hellspite," ordered the Scarecrow.

Mipps reloaded and fired again. This time the splash was within a bare three yards of the Frenchman, who replied insolently with a roaring broadside.

Not a shot struck the Greyhound, for, keeping head on, she presented little enough target.

Perhaps it was then that the Frenchman saw the great spectre of the man-o'war looming in the wake of the Greyhound, for he changed his course, abandoning the pursuit of the smuggling luggers and headed back for French waters. But he was reckoning without the Greyhound.

"Bend more canvas, you jolly dogs," cried the Scarecrow. "No, no. Strike nothing. Cram on the canvas, every inch. We'll show this Frenchman how to pocket a wind."

Once more he stood by Hellspite at the gun. "Take your own good time, but when you do fire, I have a fancy to see her mast unstepped." Mipps took careful aim, hesitating as they plunged up and down upon the moonlit waves. At last he felt sure, and fired. A flash, a roar, and then the noise of rending wood like a great tree felled. And so it proved, for down came the great mast.

The French captain's voice could be heard above the

confusion, ordering his crew to cut away wreckage and clear for action.

"Like old times," said the Scarecrow to Mipps, and then, turning to his crew, cried out, "Boarding party away." The helmsman had had his orders and he ran in the uptilted bowsprit of the Greyhound across the enemy's stern.

Hidden by the jibs, the Scarecrow, followed by his boarding party, scrambled along the bowsprit and then with a wild leap he was on the Frenchman's deck with drawn sword, crying out, "A moi, Monsieur le Capitaine Delacroix. En garde!" The Frenchman, who was amidships, drew his sword with a "Qui va là?"

"Je suis l'Epouvantail," he cried.

The French crew echoed the name in fear, while the Night-riders shouted the word in English as their battle-cry: "The Scarecrow!" But the French captain was brave enough. Telling his men to leave it to him, he rushed aft and met Syn blade to blade. Behind his back Syn's men, armed with pistols and cutlasses, formed a semi-circle, while the Frenchmen formed the like behind their leader.

"Don't fire," ordered the Admiral on the Vengeance. "Let the rascals kill each other if they wish, and then we will take our prizes."

"Don't fire," ordered Syn to the men behind him.

The vessels were drifting slowly together, for the Night-riders had thrown out grappling-irons, but the helmsman on the Greyhound was not idle.

Straining against the great tiller, he brought the locked vessels slowly but surely away from beneath the threatening guns of the man-o'-war. Meanwhile on the deck of the privateer the blades of the two swordsmen hissed and clashed like lightning in the moonlight. The steel slithered like quicksilver.

Twice was the Frenchman beaten to the bulwarks, and twice, as though not willing yet to terminate so good a fight, the tall Scarecrow retreated, encouraging his adversary to a fresh effort.

"They fight like a couple of gentlemen, the rascals," admitted the watching Admiral.

And then the end came. A howl of triumph from the Scarecrow that rang out into the night, and the Frenchman's sword whirled into the air and fell into the sea. An irrepressible cheer rang out from the man-o'-war's men, for, as they said, the rascally victor was at least British.

The cheer was a signal for a general melée. Pistols flashed.

Cutlasses, belaying-pins and hand-spikes joined in the grim struggle. The French captain, who had been seized by two burly Dymchurch men, yet roared out encouragement to his men, but they were no match for the men of Romney Marsh, and in a few minutes were crying out for quarter.

This the Scarecrow allowed immediately, telling them in their own tongue to lay down their arms. When this was done he ordered those who could swim to step to the bulwarks. Some dozen obeyed. They could swim well enough, they said, expecting that the rest were to be put to death out of hand. Those who could not swim looked at the jumbled waters and trembled.

"Then prick 'em overboard, lads," cried the Scarecrow. "They'll be picked up by the men on the Vengeance. It's a way they have in the British Navy."

The swimmers did not wait to be pricked over but jumped for it.

"Walkin' the plank, eh?" chuckled Mipps, who had followed his master along the bowsprit. "And what now, sir?" Syn whispered quickly into the sexton's ear, finishing his orders with "Understand?" But Mipps with consternation on his face cried out, "Oh no, not that. It's madness."

"It's orders," rasped Syn.

"Aye, aye, sir," replied Mipps quietly.

"You see," went on Syn in a kinder tone, "I have always felt a little sorry for General Troubridge. The Scarecrow has treated him damned shabbily on the whole, and I would like to give him cause to laugh back at his twin brother the Admiral."

A boat was accordingly lowered and Captain Delacroix was told to step into it under guard. The Scarecrow sprang in last and ordered the four oarsmen to pull for the Vengeance. Meanwhile the sailors on the man-o'-war were busy rescuing the swimming Frenchmen.

"I knew they would, and I wanted to give them something to do," chuckled Syn.

As they pulled alongside the Vengeance, the Scarecrow stood up in the stern sheets and hailed. "The Scarecrow is bringing aboard Captain Delacroix to be tried by the High Court of Admiralty for stealing our tubs. May we come aboard?" Upon the officer of the watch bawling out assent, the Scarecrow made fast the hanging rope ladder and, bowing to the Frenchman, asked him to climb first, following himself immediately behind. As soon as they were on the rope, the boat, according to instructions, pulled away. The officer of the watch never having been placed in such a position seemed a little uncertain of what he should do, but the moment the Scarecrow climbed aboard, that grotesquelooking person took the ordering upon himself. "Your servant, sir," he said gruffly. "Kindly conduct me and my prisoner to the Admiral." The Admiral met them on the quarter-deck. "My prisoner, sir," said the Scarecrow. "And since I speak his tongue I have taken the liberty of assuring him that he will be treated as an officer and gallant foe while under your command." The Admiral bowed to Captain Delacroix and gave orders for him to be taken below under guard. "As for you, sir," he continued, addressing the Scarecrow, "since for once you have shown yourself on the side of the authorities, I will ask you to step into my cabin and take a glass of wine with me, though I regret that you must consider yourself my prisoner. I see that you are still wearing your sword, which you use well, but I must ask for it."

The Scarecrow drew his sword and bowed. He heard an order behind him followed by the noise of cutlasses being drawn.

"I agree with you, sir," he replied, "that I have this night done some service to the Admiralty by ridding the Channel of an enemy privateer. I regret I cannot drink with you, as time presses, but I will so far humour your hospitality.

Within the week I will return to inquire after my prisoner, and then I will very gladly drink your good health." As he spoke he bowed and backed. Then turning like a tiger, his sword met the drawn cutlasses behind him. One honest sailor dropped his with a curse and the blood streaming from his forearm, and the other blades were turned aside as the weird figure leapt to the bulwarks and jumped overboard.

Admiral, Captain, officers and men rushed to the side, while a Marine officer snatched a musket from one of his men.

"No!" cried the Admiral. "No firing. 'Fore God, I'd rather look a fool ashore than shoot a brave man swimming." Meanwhile with strong strokes the Scarecrow was seen cresting the waves and being hauled aboard his boat.

"About ship!" roared the Admiral. "Then give 'em a warning shot, and if they don't heave to, after 'em." But they were reckoning without Sexton Mipps and his former knowledge of the sea. He had been very busy in his master's absence, so that by the time the great seventy-four swung round the Scarecrow was aboard the Greyhound, which, full canvas set and a cable towing the partially disabled privateer in her wake, was gathering speed and wind in favour.

"Good little devil," cried the dripping Scarecrow, clapping Mipps on the back. "We'll slip that cable if necessary, but we'll find the privateer a useful addition to our smuggling fleet. We've got the start, and we'll keep it so long as we keep out of line of fire. Keep dead ahead of her and tack whenever she swings." Once only did the guns of the Vengeance roar out after the warning shot, but whether the gunners were in sympathy with the Scarecrow's daring or not, it is certain that the salvo fell short, and the flag-ship returned to Dover harbour next morning with the prize of one French captain.

A week later Doctor Syn once more looked up the rope ladder that hung from the side of H.M.S. Vengeance. This time no sea was running. The harbour was like a mirror. He turned, however, to the sailors who had rowed him out to be entertained by his friend Admiral Troubridge, and shaking his head said:

"You don't expect me to climb up that thing, surely. I simply could not do it."

"All right, sir," replied the sailor. "He, there! Let down the gamming chair."

"What?" replied a sailor of the watch.

"Shove down an Admiral's cradle. A gamming stool. The reverend gentleman don't like ropes." Down came a cushioned chair with no legs, but hanging straps. Doctor Syn was strapped in. "Right away for heaven then," cried the sailor. The poor parson, swinging round and round, was hoisted on to deck and conducted to the Admiral, who told him that the Scarecrow had swarmed up that very ropeladder with a heavy swell running.

"But for all that," said the Admiral, after recounting his adventure, "I am disappointed in the rascal. He told me he would take wine with me within the week, and I've kept this bottle on purpose. Well, he won't come now, so let me pour you out a glass."

"I rather expect he was just bragging, don't you, sir?" said the parson.

"Aye," replied the Admiral. "He'll never dare come aboard again and drink with me. But for all that, I rather thought he would."

"Allow something for a bragging rascal," smiled the parson, holding up his glass. "In any case you caught the Frenchman."

"And got no glory for it," retorted the sea-dog. "Every sailor aboard went ashore telling the facts as they happened, making the Scarecrow more of a hero than ever. However, as I say, he's not quite the man I thought him. He has not dared to come to my cabin and sample this sherry."

"Well, in his stead, let me drink your very good health, sir," replied Doctor Syn, who had at least the private satisfaction of knowing that the Scarecrow was no braggart, but he thought it wiser to keep such knowledge to himself.

Chapter 14. Doctor Syn arranges a duel

General Troubridge was not in favour of his officers duelling. He gave Major Faunce strict orders to watch over such "affairs of honour", and unless the cause was such that no gentleman could refrain from "going out", the argument was brought to the General, who acted as peacemaker. Consequently the Dragoons did not fight over such trifles as the correct set of a cravat, nor for any so-called insult over the critical points of a favourite horse or dog. But when the quarrel touched the honour of a lady, why, then the General showed the romantic side of his humanity. He never attempted to stop an affair of honour connected with the officers under him when he learnt that the aggressor had offered insult to the mother, wife, sister or sweetheart of one of his Dragoons. "Go and wing him, sir. Go and spit him, sir," he would cry, "and may God defend the right and a Gentleman Dragoon." Now it chanced that a certain officer of a certain regiment of Foot was appointed to a command in Dover Castle. This slim, elegant, though cadaverous fellow went by the rank and name of Captain Raikes. His worst enemy was ready to own that Raikes was a wizard with steel or lead, but would whisper behind his back that never had there been such an evil, cantankerous prince of cats in the British Army. Raikes was a rich man who had travelled widely on the Continent, and had spent much money at the various fencing academies, till he had become the very butcher of a silk button, which his point could pick off with the dexterity of a quick-job tailor. With his a sword fight could be safely continued just so long as it amused him, but whenever it pleased him to terminate further exertion, it was but "one", "two" and the "third" in your bosom.

This undesirable quarreler became acquainted with Troubridge's Dragoons, and feeling, no doubt, the inferiority of the infantry to the acknowledged superiority of the cavalry, went immediately to find occasion for proving that a Captain of Foot could excel any hard-riding Dragoon in the subtleties of the sword or the flight of a bullet.

Knowing the terrible reputation of this man of blood, General Troubridge trembled for the safety of his high-spirited young officers, and put Major Faunce the more on his guard. Perhaps Captain Raikes thought the better of the Dragoons by reason of the tact and skill with which they avoided a meeting with him, and to think the better of anyone was, in the heart of Captain Raikes, to wish a different opinion, which would not be difficult, he knew, if he could but get one of them to face him on the greensward.

Now through information retrieved from spies of the Customs that the Scarecrow was planning another of his colossal contraband runs, the Dragoons were ordered from Canterbury and billeted upon the Foot Regiment at Dover Castle. At the time of the Dragoons' arrival Captain Raikes was Officer of the Mess, and although responsible for his guests' comfort, found that he could as easily irritate them in many little ways. However, thanks to the General's warning and Major Faunce's vigilance, the cavalry officers pretended neither to notice his sneers nor to comprehend his offensive remarks.

And then came the affair of the Garrison Ball, which gave Bully Raikes the opportunity he had been seeking.

Everyone in the neighbourhood that could boast rank or gentility was invited, and Captain Raikes was appointed by his Colonel to undertake the onerous duty of Master of Ceremonies. No doubt the good Colonel thought that the very obligation of such an office would force the quarrelsome Captain to behave himself. In this he was mistaken, for Raikes was determined to make the evening an occasion for fixing a quarrel with one of the Dragoons, and the man he picked upon as the most delectable to quarrel with was young Brackenbury, a handsome officer who had recently been promoted to a captaincy, and was the fortunate husband of Sir Henry Pembury's youngest daughter Kate.

That night it was not only her husband and her father, the Lord of Lympne, but every fair-minded man and woman too in the ballroom who voted her the most beautiful in all that galaxy of beauty. Raikes thought so too, and in his conceit imagined that he could easily gain a double conquest against the hated Dragoons by killing the husband and in time ruining the wife. What was only meant for a smile of the purest courtesy from her kind, ladylike and pure eyes he translated as something more intriguing, something indeed of invitation, which any gentleman knowing Kate Brackenbury would have known was not possible to such a peerless girl.

In this Raikes' experience showed itself misinformed and most lamentably ignorant. As Master of Ceremonies he claimed the right to dance with her once, and dared to whisper something which brought the blush of shame to her cheeks. He misinterpreted that blush and his ignorance of purity plunged him only the further into error. Her exquisite beauty had caught his imagination, and he blundered on to what was eventually to prove his great disaster.

The scene of his disaster was in one of the large card-rooms adjoining the dancing floor. It was during an interval between play, and the Master of Ceremonies was well within his rights to enter in order to persuade the guests to take their promised partners for the next quadrille. Sir Henry Pembury and his daughter were talking to a group of Dragoon officers, amongst whom were General Troubridge and Captain Brackenbury.

Raikes approached them with, "By my faith, gentlemen, but 'tis ill taste of you to hold a council of war when your fair partners are waiting to be led out for the quadrille. Are you sharing condolences that by this time tomorrow your regiment will no doubt be once more the laughing-stock of this low-bred smuggler, the Scarecrow? 'Fore Gad, if I don't forfeit my night's rest and ride out to see the fun. I imagine that the Scarecrow is looking forward to it rather more than yourselves." Then turning to Kate Brackenbury, and eyeing her through his quizzing-glass, he added, "But the contemplation of yet another disaster to your husband's regiment cannot be very entertaining to you, Madame. I therefore offer you my hand to conduct you to something more lively: to wit, the fiddles and quadrille."

"My remaining dances for the evening have already been promised, Captain Raikes," she answered coldly.

"And who has the honour of this one, may I ask?" demanded the Captain.

"If you must know, sir, my husband, Captain Brackenbury," she retorted.

"Oh, sink me, no!" replied Raikes. "As Master of Ceremonies I refuse to allow such a pretty girl to be bored with her own husband, and I am sure he will reasonably and no doubt gladly release you."

"I thank you, sir," was the icy reply, "but I have no wish to be released—"

"Any more than I have, sir," added young Brackenbury with an angry flush.

Endeavouring to wither the bully with a look of extreme contempt, General Troubridge rapped out: "If in your position of our host you have anything to say to us, sir, I beg that you will do so and withdraw. Sir Henry here will bear me out that we were making use of this card-room to indulge in a little private conversation."

"I can guess the trend of it," laughed Raikes. "No doubt you were laying out a plan of campaign to avoid open fight with the Scarecrow's men, eh?"

Sir Henry Pembury, though secure enough by reason of age, gout and his position as magistrate, stepped up to Raikes and said bravely, "I rather think, sir, that you are forgetting your manners in the presence of my daughter." Young Brackenbury also took a step forward and added, "I suggest, Sir Henry, that Captain Raikes could hardly forget what he has so obviously never learnt."

"And I suggest something entirely different, and certainly more droll," said a kind, sweet voice from the door behind the back of the bully Captain, who turned and confronted the neat black-frocked figure of Doctor Syn, Vicar of Dymchurch.

"I don't know that we are very anxious to hear your suggestion, reverend sir, however droll," sneered Raikes, furious that his opportunity of calling out Brackenbury was for the moment postponed.

"Now look you, sir," went on Doctor Syn amiably. "Although I cannot say with any particle of truth that any of us have ever heard the smallest thing about you in your favour, my profession compels me ever to put the best complexion upon man or beast, and under whichever category you may be classed, I promise you that I shall feel myself obligated to do you what justice is possible for what I fear is a very bad case. Apart from my duty to my cloth, I confess that I dislike you intensely, as I verily believe every other honest man must do, but still for all that I—"

"Hold your damned interfering tongue, you old fool," interrupted Captain Raikes. "Your cloth offers you protection which you are using to unfair advantage. One treats a parson as one does a woman—"

"With the full use of your ill-breeding, sir?" suggested Doctor Syn.

"Sink me, sir," retorted the bully hotly, "but you are taking an unfair advantage—"

"A practice which I understand you so often do yourself," put in the parson mildly.

"You know very well that I cannot challenge you," cried out Raikes.

"I fail to see why not, unless it is that you are as cowardly as I think you to be," smiled Doctor Syn. "But let me remind you," he went on pleasantly, "that if you do so far honour me, that it is my province to choose the weapons, and have you any idea what they would be? No? Well, I will tell you. Like any other bully—and I confess that there is as much of the bully in me as there is in you —I should choose the best weapon for my own advantage, and a weapon which I venture to think I am a greater exponent of than yourself, unless you have been, like I have, an Oxford tutor. I warn you, sir, that this experience has taught me to wield the birch with very good effect, and as they say that to spare the rod is to spoil the child, I will promise not to spoil you."

"Do you imagine, sir, for one moment that a Captain of Foot, who has fought in affairs of honour all over the world, would fight or even bandy words with a doddering old parson?" The rage of Captain Raikes was the further increased since he was well aware that the Dragoon officers were enjoying this wrangle.

"Quite honestly, sir," replied Doctor Syn, "I should not be surprised to hear you deny to fight anyone unless you felt entirely safe in doing so, and that brings me to what I called my droll suggestion. Suppose you make good your words about tomorrow night. Suppose you forgo your sleep and ride out to Romney Marsh in order to witness, as you mentioned, the discomfiture of these gallant Dragoons. Suppose, with your superior tactics of war, you locate this Scarecrow yourself and repeat to him some sort of the remarks we have heard you make of him tonight. Let me see, what was it? I think you called him a lowbred smuggler. Although never having met the gentleman face to face, I suppose I must look upon him as one of my parishioners, and, however villainous the rascal is, take an interest in him. I wonder whether you would repeat your words to his face now, eh?"

"What is all this rigmarole aiming at?" demanded Raikes.

"Just this," continued the Doctor. "You have the reputation of knowing a little about fence. Well, from all I hear, this low-bred smuggler gave a very gentlemanly account of himself when his sword met that of the famous French privateer, Captain Delacroix, who owned at his trial that he counted it no shame to be disarmed by such a gallant swordsman. 'A gallant swordsman' is something more polite than the term you used, 'a low-bred smuggler'. Now, granted first that we are most anxious to rid our Marshes of this impudent fellow, and granted also that this neighbourhood is also anxious to rid itself of your cowardly conceit, my droll suggestion is that you challenge the Scarecrow and either kill him or let him kill you, so that this fair part of Kent may at least be rid of one very dirty scoundrel."

"Could I come face to face with the rascal," cried out Raikes, "I would certainly show these tardy Dragoons how to deal with a law-breaker."

"Good!" exclaimed the parson. "You hear, gentlemen? Captain Raikes has expressed his willingness to fight the Scarecrow. The only difficulty is, how is this to be accomplished? None of us know who the Scarecrow is. However, I rather think that if we spread the news of this challenge, the Scarecrow's spies, who seem to be here, there and everywhere, will inform their elusive master, and I cannot imagine that the Scarecrow will deny himself the pleasure of running Captain Raikes through the body."

"Beware of making rash promises, Captain Raikes," put in the General.

"There are many who affirm that this Scarecrow is possessed of supernatural powers, and who knows he may even now be overhearing you. Are you quite sure that you have the courage to face as good a swordsman as you are yourself?"

"Supernatural powers?" echoed Raikes. "You would think so. A very pretty excuse too for your failure to keep him in Dover Castle. But I assure you that I have no fear even of the devil himself."

"Very comforting for you," sighed Doctor Syn. "For I think there is very little doubt but that you and the devil will be boon companions when it is your turn to leave this world."

"Now look you here, reverend sir," retorted Raikes. "My patience is none of the best—"

"Nor mine, sir," smiled the parson. "I hear the fiddlers inviting us to the quadrille, and whereas Captain Brackenbury was naturally disinclined for you to lead out his wife, I am sure he will release her to me. Come, my dear Kate. I promised you that I would try to dance just once, if you would pilot me. By your leave, gentlemen. Oh, and, Raikes, my good fellow, if you meet this Scarecrow of ours, be warned. They say his face and figure are positively terrifying. Ask Major Faunce there, who has seen him. Ask Captain Brackenbury, who has actually captured him. Horrible, most horrible, they lead me to understand. So don't be frightened, will you? "Now, my dear Kate, for the quadrille," chuckled the parson, "I confess that I feel very frightened of cutting a comical figure, but at least I am proud of my partner." And so, to the tune of the fiddles, Doctor Syn led Kate Brackenbury out into the ballroom. Ignoring Raikes, Sir Henry and the General followed, while the laughing Dragoons brought up the rear.

Raikes, however, knowing that he had cut the poorest figure, pulled Brackenbury by the sleeve, saying: "You will give me satisfaction, sir, for your gross insult. I can only presume that you arranged for that fool parson to come along with his insults in the nick of time to save you from meeting me. But that will not do, sir. I shall expect to hear from you."

"Very well, sir," assented Brackenbury bravely, though in his heart he knew that he was doomed.

"The choice of weapons is with you," went on Raikes. "I presume that even a Dragoon will fight like a gentleman and not insist on being mounted and armed with a clumsy sabre."

"I will take no advantage of a mere infantryman," replied Brackenbury, with a stiff bow. "Neither will I chance to the flight of a bullet. It will be swords, sir, and if I lose, I shall at least have done my best to rid the Army of a very pretty scoundrel." And with another bow he joined his brother officers.

Half an hour later a sergeant on duty approached Captain Raikes.

"A letter, sir, addressed to the Master of Ceremonies."

"Who brought it?" asked Raikes.

"No one, sir. One of the sentries happened to see it lying on the porch steps." Raikes opened it and read:

Doctor Syn, who is no friend to me, but rather my sworn enemy by reason of his friendship with the Dragoons, told you my spies are everywhere. He was correct. I have already heard that you have publicly styled me "a low-bred smuggler", and have challenged me. I take you up. If you dare face devils and dangers, be at Botolph's Bridge upon Romney Marsh by tomorrow midnight, where one of my Night-riders will await you and arrange matters. I choose swords, and there will be lanterns as well as the full moon. You may bring a second, if you can find one to act for you. I think we may dispense with a surgeon. An undertaker would be more to the purpose.

This was not the only mysterious letter found that night, for as a very wretched Brackenbury handed his wife into Sir Henry's coach, Doctor Syn, who was of their party for the return journey, noticed a paper sealed with a plain wafer upon the seat. It was addressed to Captain Brackenbury, who read it by the light of the coach lamp.

Sir, no reflection upon your skill as a swordsman, but Raikes is a bad butcher. If you would satisfy your honour, and yet live to witness the discomfiture of Raikes, make your appointment a quarter of an hour before midnight at Botolph's Bridge. If you do this, your lady wife will not be deprived by a brute of a very gallant husband.

(Signed) The Scarecrow.

"What is it, dear?" asked Kate.

"A note of hand for a card debt which I forgot to collect," lied the Captain, for he had not told his wife of the peril he was in.

"You will do what the note says," whispered Doctor Syn, who had been shown the message. "For this Scarecrow has a finer sense of honour than your antagonist. For Kate's sake, I beg you to obey." Back in his study at Dymchurch, Doctor Syn found his faithful Sexton Mipps awaiting orders. Having informed him of the bad business connected with Raikes, Doctor Syn completed arrangements for the next night's "run".

"I have persuaded the General that his best plan will be to ambush on the sea-wall and attack the smugglers as they land the tubs on Dymchurch sands.

At the same time the Sandgate Revenue cutter is to attack from the sea. Now there will be no unloading upon Dymchurch sands. Let the luggers approach shore about midnight, appear to be suspicious, put to sea again and land the goods when the cutter has gone, upon the far side of Dungeness. This will keep the Dragoons well occupied during my business at Botolph's Bridge, where I hope to show our Night-riders some very pretty sword-play as well as giving this Raikes a lesson which he is not likely to forget."

Chapter 15. In the ring of demons

With the shadow of death upon him, as all thought, it was not difficult for young Brackenbury to obtain leave from duty, so that soon after the Dragoons had left for Dymchurch he was free to ride by a different route for Botolph's Bridge. It was a cold night with a clear moon. Never had young Brackenbury felt so cut off from the world as he viewed that desolate scene while awaiting his antagonist. For the sake of secrecy they had agreed to fight without seconds and to the death.

The eeriness of that empty Marsh robbed the young officer of all hope. Even the Scarecrow could not save him, for the only moving figure on that wide expanse was Death on Horseback, in the shape of the dreaded Captain Raikes as he trotted towards him along the winding road. The inn by the bridge was dark and close-shuttered. There could be no hope from there, for he was quite sure that its inhabitants and cronies would be far away upon the Scarecrow's business. In a dream he saw the cadaverous Raikes dismount, strip off his riding coat, his vest, roll up his sleeves, look at his fob-watch and scan the Marsh before drawing his sword. In the same dream Brackenbury found that he had done the same, except that his last act, after viewing the time from his fobwatch, was to say a prayer towards the distant heights of Lympne, where in the Castle slept his adorable wife, little realizing that her husband was about to go to death, unless the Scarecrow could perform a miracle.

"We will fence a little first to warm us up," laughed Raikes.

"I came here to fight, sir, not to fence," replied the other coldly.

The moment they came on guard Brackenbury attacked furiously, so that Raikes actually had to retreat, which he did with a sneer of amusement on his face. "A gentleman should keep his temper even in a fight," he said, and then without effort he began to drive back the younger man.

It was then that above the ring of the swords there arose, as from the very bowels of the Marsh, a cry, loud and piercing, as of a thousand devils.

Brackenbury saw a look of terror in his enemy's eyes, and this same terror seemed to arrest his sword-arm. This happened as

Brackenbury was making a desperate lunge, and unable to check himself the young man felt his point prick into the other's forearm. Raikes stood still and stared at something behind Brackenbury, who panted out: "I apologize. I did not intend a mean advantage."

"Look," whispered Raikes. "In God's name—"

"No, in the devil's name, Mister Butcher Raikes," cried out a fierce raucous voice. Brackenbury turned and saw a long length of unnatural light shining up from what appeared to be a deep crack in the earth, while above it, as though risen from hell, sat the wild, black, ragged figure of the Scarecrow astride his fierce black steed. At the same time another wild yell of derision arose from the supernatural light, and from it there appeared some fifty ghastly figures— witches and demons.

Out from the deep dry dyke in which they had been concealed, they rode on fantastically trapped horses, and waving their jack-o'-lanterns above their heads, they galloped round the field, closing in a circle around the mazed duellists. Then into that circle of light rode the Scarecrow, with a drawn sword in his hand. Leaping from his horse, his raucous voice croaked through the hideous mask: "Captain Brackenbury, your honour can rest satisfied. You have drawn first blood. In any case, I, the Scarecrow, have first claim to meet this butcher's sword, for he challenged me before he challenged you. So, on guard, Butcher. On guard, and enjoy your last fight for some time." The Scarecrow leapt forward and Raikes had barely time to guard himself.

Brackenbury confessed afterwards that he was almost sorry for Raikes. He had no chance. The horror of the scene unnerved him. Surrounded by ghastly devils that shrieked with glee at his discomfiture, he was driven round and round in that circle by the Scarecrow's blade, and was unable to cope with a vehemence he had never before experienced.

Twice he fell, and twice was ordered up, only to be driven backwards again by the lightning steel, until at last he went down amidst a howl of derision, while the Scarecrow wiped his sword upon his ragged cloak, saying: "I had a mind to pass it through his heart instead of his shoulder, but this will keep him quiet, I fancy, for a long time. Where's Hellspite?"

A little man dressed as a devil came forward and opened a box of surgical appliances, from which the Scarecrow skilfully dressed the wound. "Ready for the cart," said the Scarecrow when this was done, and into the circle came an old vegetable cart driven by a yokel muffled up to the eyes. "Captain Brackenbury," he went on, "we are returning him with these other vegetables to his regiment, while you will be escorted back to Lympne, for I cannot afford to let you communicate with the Dragoons tonight. But you may tell your General in the morning that while his troopers were guarding Dymchurch Wall the Scarecrow carried out a most profitable run upon the further side of Dungeness.

Lead the Captain to his horse. This Raikes will forfeit his, and his charger shall turn pack pony. And now for Dungeness." As he was led away, Brackenbury saw the Scarecrow pick up Raikes' sword, snap it across his knee and throw it broken into the cart, where Raikes was being covered with the contents of many vegetable baskets.

The next morning a yokel unharnessed his cart-horse before the cookhouse of Dover Castle. "Goin' to get him shod. I'll come back for the cart," he said.

But that he never did, and when the pile of cabbages was removed they uncovered the half-conscious body of Raikes. His broken sword lay beside him, and a notice was pinned to his coat: "VEGETABLES—WITH THE SCARECROW'S COMPLIMENTS". And a few days later Doctor Syn chuckled to himself when he heard that Captain Raikes had resigned his commission and left the neighbourhood.

Chapter 16. The clue of the gilt button

In the days of Doctor Syn very few villages could boast of more prosperity than Dymchurch-under-the-wall. The Vicar himself was a man of some means and very generous. Besides, on behalf of a needy parishioner he could always draw on the wealth of Sir Antony Cobtree, who was the class of squire who took a personal interest in his tenants' welfare.

Yet none knew better than the Squire and the Vicar that the chief local benefactor was the notorious Scarecrow. Indeed Doctor Syn would sometimes remark whimsically that the leader of the Romney Marsh smugglers had his uses, for despite his rogueries he was at least a considerable employer of labour, putting more money into the farmers' pockets than their farms could possibly produce, and more into the fishermen's pockets than their best catches could warrant.

Therefore a poor man upon the Marsh was looked upon as either lazy or untrustworthy, for, what with the generosity of the Squire, the Vicar and the Scarecrow, there was plenty of money to be earned. And such a man was Craigen, a tall powerful brute, who preferred drinking money to earning it. He was a small-part owner in a sailing vessel with the two Evendens, one of whom, John, had married Craigen's sister. Although John and his brother Edmond took by far the greater shares, they allowed Craigen, by reason of his relationship, a proportionate allowance on each catch, these catches being more often tubs than fish, for the Evendens trafficked in contraband, and were the only smugglers that had not been co-operated into the Scarecrow's gang. The Evendens would have made far more money had they joined under the banner of the smuggling genius, but they were obstinate men who preferred to go their own way.

As for Craigen, the Scarecrow would have no dealings with him at all, sending him the whimsical message that a man for whom neither Church nor State had any respect was not a fit man to ride with his Night Demons of the Marsh. Hence it was that the crew of the Evenden boat had no liking for the Scarecrow.

Craigen had no liking for anyone but himself, and hated particularly any more prosperous. He therefore included his brothers-in-law in his vast list of enemies, and for a long time he had contemplated the possibility of getting rid of them by violent means. No sooner had this crime become an obsession in his drunken brain than he took steps to put it into operation. Being a drunken blunderer, he was bound to slip up on his very first step, for, thinking that his sister had gone to Folkestone with her husband, when she had only gone into Hythe market, she walked into her bedroom, the door of which he had neglected to lock, and discovered him dressed in the Sunday suit of her husband and surveying the fit in the cracked pier-glass.

"What on earth are you doing in John's best clothes?" she demanded angrily.

"Only satisfying myself about a bet, so don't take on," replied Craigen sheepishly. "A lying rogue at the Ship Inn told me that your John was a finer set-up man than myself, and that his clothes would flap around me. I said John was a fine figure of a man certainly, but that we were both of a size, and I just thought as how I'd prove the man a liar by trying on John's suit, see? No harm in that, considering the rogue is willing to bet a shilling on it. And look here, lass, if you say nothing to John, who we know is hot-tempered over trifles, I'll give you a silver fourpenny out of the money when I win it."

"I want none of your dirty money," snapped his sister. "You put them clothes back where you found 'em, and never dare to come into our bedroom again."

"You won't be so gross-grained when you see the shining fourpenny," laughed Craigen. "Get downstairs while I change into my own comfortable clothes. I never did hold with John trying to dress on Sundays like the gentry. A smuggler didn't ought to go to church, I say." Down the ladder stairway went his sister, snorting indignation. She waited for her brother, however, in the kitchen below, for she was determined to see for herself that he took nothing out with him. She had missed things before when her rogue brother was short of money and craved for drink.

In this case Craigen proved too cunning for her. Wanting the clothes for another purpose to what he had said, he tied them in a bundle and dropped them out of the casement behind a gooseberry bush. Then, closing the drawer from which he had taken them with as much noise as possible, he came downstairs, saying: "There you are, lass, and no harm done. Now that I can see we are of a size, I'll take on his bet and get Mr. Mipps to measure us up with his coffin rule. I only bet on what I'm sure on, see? Keep it to yourself and you'll get your silver bit." She shut the door after him, so that he was able to go round the house and collect this bundle without being seen. After taking the clothes to his own cottage he went to the Ship Inn, where he began to spend his savings in rum, telling everyone that he needed cheering up after hearing his two brothers-inlaw quarrelling so badly. When turned out by Mrs. Waggetts, the landlady, as having drunk enough, he went to the City of London, from which premises he was soon warned off as being in no fit state for more, and then for the rest of the day he hid himself in one of the high-backed seats of the Ocean Tavern.

Here he had the sense to behave himself, knowing that he needed all the drink he could get in order to put courage into his cowardly soul for what he had planned to do. When he left the Ocean that night he had the satisfaction of knowing that in each inn he had visited he had at least spread the lying news that there was the worst blood between the Evenden brothers, and that the quarrel he had witnessed was likely to end in bad results.

Knowing that John Evenden had gone into Folkestone to make an arrangement for a hide of tubs, and that his brother Edmond would be going down to the boat with the nets which he had been mending, he had marked out Edmond as the victim for his purpose. This fitted in well with his diabolical scheme. He, Craigen, would wear John's suit, so that if there were blood-spots on his clothes it would be John, and not himself, that would be implicated. He knew Edmond's habit of bringing the nets down into the cabin without a light, so he cut away three rungs of the rough ladder from the deck, and with his knife ready, waited for Edmond to stumble down. Then all he had to do was to depend upon rum-soaked courage to leap forward upon his fallen victim, and with a resolute stroke of the knife Edmond would be no more.

Thanks to his lies about the quarrel and the bloodstains on the clothes, John Evenden would be hanged and he, Craigen, would gain sole ownership of the boat, which with ill-paid hands would gain him large profit, for he knew all the people in France with whom his relatives had dealt. So, primed to courage with rum, Craigen waited in the darkness of the cabin.

Now it happened that John Evenden returned earlier than he thought possible from Folkestone. His wife had elected to sit up late in order to do some neglected mending, so that he found her downstairs when he came home.

"Not yet abed, my lass?" he asked. "I have done a profitable deal. Better than I thought."

"I had some sewing to do," replied his wife.

"And you shall not be at a loss for that," returned John heartily. "I have done well, and my deal has brought me many a guinea in advance. We are to fish tomorrow night off Grisnez, and a French lugger is to come alongside in neutral waters. We are to hide what the ships aboard us beneath a wriggling cargo of live fish. Now, had you been lazily abed you might have got nothing out of my good fortune, but since I find you a hard-working lass, you shall have five good golden guineas for yourself." Whereupon he produced the money, which she straightway put into the tea-caddy.

"And finding you at your mending," went on John, "puts me in mind of something. My Sunday suit is all but losing one of its fine gilt buttons. So while I indulge in a pipe of my best Virginian, will you lash it on taut for me? But, first tell me, where's my brother Edmond?"

"He's gone down to the boat with the mended nets," explained his wife.

Then she climbed up the ladder to the bedroom to fetch the Sunday coat.

Her husband heard her open the drawer in which his suit was kept, and although he did not know it, it was at that very second that Edmond stumbled on the boat's ladder, slipped and fell on to the cabin floor of the family boat, where he received six inches of steel through his heart.

"The suit is gone!" Mrs. Evenden cried out.

"Gone?" repeated her husband. "Oh, nonsense." White-faced and tight-lipped his wife came down into the kitchen. Five guineas from her husband ruled out any doubtful obligation of a silver fourpenny from her brother, who would surely neglect to give it her. He never kept his word. Besides, she had never given hers. So Mrs. Evenden told her husband of Craigen's impertinence concerning the Sunday suit, adding significantly: "And now it's gone. What does it mean?" As if in answer there came a very decided rapping upon the door. Had they known, they might have put down the sudden terror which gripped them to the fact that Edmond had just gone to a sudden death and had come to warn them. It was not till the rapping was repeated that they opened the door to find Doctor Syn standing there.

"Forgive the lateness of the hour for a visit," he said, "but I have been visiting sick folk in the parish, and have heard gossip that has distressed me. Is it true, John Evenden, that you have been quarrelling with your brother Edmond?"

"Good gracious, no, sir," laughed John, ushering the kindly Vicar into the parlour. "Whoever said a thing like that?" Doctor Syn did not tell him that his faithful Sexton Mipps had given him the report. Nor did he tell him that he had given Mipps instructions to watch the Evendens and Craigen on behalf of the Scarecrow's interests. And then, since everybody in Dymchurch trusted the tact and confidence of their Vicar, Mrs. Evenden told him of the incident connected with the Sunday suit. Now John hated Craigen, and only tolerated him for his wife's sake, but he loved his brother Edmond.

Perhaps it was the hearing of the story the second time that prompted him, or, as Mrs. Evenden afterwards believed, it may have been that Edmond's spirit was permitted to communicate with him, but John Evenden gave a sudden gasp of horror, and then, seizing Doctor Syn's hands, cried out: "For God's sake, sir, bide here a bit with the wife. I am going to the boat. Edmond went there. He's calling me as though for help. I'm afraid, sir. I'm afraid." Doctor Syn stayed with Mrs. Evenden and did his best to allay her fears, though John had gone, blundering to his death, like his brother. It was Mipps who brought them the ill tidings within the hour. Ill tidings to Mrs. Evenden, who learned that both her husband and brother-in-law had been foully murdered, and ill tidings to Doctor Syn when Mipps produced two badly written scrawls on papers which he had taken from the stabbed bodies of the Evendens. Doctor Syn read the scrawled message and frowned: "BY VENGEANCE OF THE SCARECROW." Mipps had persuaded the beadle to let him take these papers to the Vicar, who might be able to identify the writing, since he had seen specimens of it before. "But it don't look like the Scarecrow's fist to me, Vicar," said Mipps, "and so I says to the beadle. But the beadle, he says, 'The Scarecrow would disguise his writing,' he says, 'when it comes to a matter of murder.' All the same I says that I don't hold the opinion that the Scarecrow did these murders."

"No more do I, Mipps," replied the Vicar. "The murderer thinks to put the blame on him, that's clear. Whoever the Scarecrow may be, this night's work looks an awkward business for him, however innocent he may be of it. True, some of our Dymchurch lads will wink at a little cargo-running, but there's none of them would countenance murder."

"Where is my brother?" asked Mrs. Evenden suddenly.

"Ah," replied Mipps. "He's down there now answering questions off of the beadle, who sent to his cottage and had him routed out. They took some time to wake him too, him having had more drink than he could carry. And was it true that your husband had quarrelled so fierce with his brother, like what Craigen says?"

"It was a wicked lie," replied Mrs. Evenden. "Why, John had been into Folkestone and had not seen Edmond all day. Doctor Syn will bear me out in that, since he had only returned a few minutes before the Vicar came in." Doctor Syn believed her, and after leaving her with a neighbour, he accompanied Mipps to the scene of the crime. The bodies were lying side by side on the thwarts of the Evenden boat. Old Sennacherib Pepper, the Dymchurch physician, had pronounced life to be extinct in both cases. While the bodies were attracting the attention of the fast-increasing crowd of morbid sightseers, Doctor Syn unobtrusively climbed down the ladder into the cabin.

He found the three rungs that had been cut away lying in a corner. By the light of the lantern he carried he examined all the cracks between the ribbed sides of the vessel and the rough decking.

Meanwhile the folk above were more interested in the corpses than in the blood-stains in the cabin, so nobody saw the Vicar stoop and pick up a large gilt button, which he slipped into his pocket. But even then he continued to search every nook and cranny of the cabin.

In contrast to the unobtrusive behaviour of Doctor Syn was that of Craigen, who hysterically proclaimed his grief with wild wringing of the hands, and bellowing out his family disaster with loud curses against the Scarecrow. His outbursts got on the nerves of Doctor Pepper, who, after seeing to the decent removal of the bodies, ordered Craigen to be escorted home, put to bed, and be given a sleeping draught which he promised to bring along.

But it chanced to be the spiritual doctor who was destined to administer the draught, for, as Doctor Syn said to Doctor Pepper, "I will take it to him and save you the journey, for it is my duty to see whether I cannot first give him a little spiritual consolation." This Doctor Syn did not attempt, but rather gave the sleeping draught to the bereaved rogue, so that he could as quickly as possible make a thorough search of his cottage, in order to find what he had failed to find in the cabin of the boat. His search was rewarded. From a hole in the ceiling of a cupboard he dragged forth what he had been seeking—the Sunday clothes of John Evenden.

The coat of it, with one button missing, was sadly bespattered with blood.

Had the Vicar there and then carried the suit to the authorities, the case against Craigen would have been complete, but it chanced that the Vicar had already made up his mind to go a very different way to work. He carried the suit to his Vicarage, and in the presence of Mipps the sexton, he shut it up in an iron chest.

"And now my good Mipps," he said, when this was done, "since it is obvious that this double murderer has tried to put a noose around our necks, well, we must use his own life, justly forfeited, to our own advantage."

"Certainly, Vicar," agreed Mipps. "Hand him over to Jack Ketch and be done with him." Syn smiled and shook his head. "On the contrary. This Craigen has done two murders, and with this monstrous accusation against the Scarecrow might have done another by the simple means of putting a noose around the Scarecrow's neck, which might have involved you too, as the Scarecrow's first lieutenant. Craigen, however, has committed blunders. We never do commit them. In fact we have the skill which he lacks. This being so, we will allow him to hand over the Scarecrow to the Dragoons. In fact the Dragoons shall have the glory of killing the Scarecrow. But always with this reservation, my excellent Mipps. The Scarecrow shall rise again before their eyes, and the resurrection shall take place before the Scarecrow's corpse is cold." Mipps scratched his head and shook it doubtfully. "I don't understand, sir," he said.

"No?" queried Syn, who loved to befog the little sexton. "Then pass the brandy. For brandy clears the stupidest head, and yours is not always stupid.

Now, your first office will be to spread the news to the Night-riders secretly that the Scarecrow did not do these murders, but that he knows already who did, and that he will forestall the law and mete out his own quick punishment.

It is good that the Scarecrow shall be feared."

"You think Craigen did 'em, eh?" asked Mipps. "But how do you know?"

"From what Mrs. Evenden told me, and from what I saw in the Evenden boat."

Chapter 17. The terror of Craigen

At the inquiry, which was duly held at the Court House, Doctor Syn gave a simple evidence, but failed to say anything about the Sunday suit, or any other thing that might point suspicion towards Craigen. Mrs. Evenden did not appear, for, as Doctor Syn pointed out, it would be too cruel to expect her.

Craigen, however, made up for her absence by giving his evidence in a storm of sobs. In fact his obvious distress went greatly in his favour. His brothers-in-law, he said, were the best of good men, and though by their death he certainly stood to gain ownership of the family fishing boat, he would that he could forgo such fortune to have his brothers-in-law alive again. In any case he declared that he would see that his sister received full share of all his profits from fishing.

Doctor Syn chuckled at heart to hear Craigen thus playing the good man, and especially since the authorities decided that the murders had indeed been committed by the Scarecrow. Amongst others who attended the proceedings was General Troubridge, who was delighted that the elusive Scarecrow had implicated himself so seriously, and he urged that the Marshes should be scoured till the miscreant was hanged. It was not till after dinner at the Squire's, however, that Doctor Syn got a chance of any private conversation with him.

"I take it, General," he whispered, "that you are still as anxious as I have ever been to rid the countryside of this Scarecrow."

"More than ever now," returned the General. "I grant that the writing on those papers is different to the other scrawled notes we have seen of the rascal's penmanship. But your beadle is right in affirming that any murderer must first disguise his writing."

"I do not quite see that," replied Doctor Syn. "Why would he wish to disguise writing that he put his name so boldly upon?"

"Ah," replied the General knowingly. "The ways of criminals are very irresponsible. I have not the slightest doubt but that the Scarecrow did murder these men. Indeed, I will go so far as to say that I shall order my men to shoot him on sight, rather than run the risk of taking him prisoner and letting him do another miraculous escape."

"Your attitude delights me," whispered the Vicar. "We are going to get him this time, I think, sir. Read this." Doctor Syn handed the General a letter which was obviously written in the up-and-down hand of the Scarecrow. It read:

Doctor Syn, you are becoming a menace to me, but I have no desire to kill a man of God, who is trusted by the worst characters on Romney Marsh. I would rather bargain with you, and you shall find that my bargaining will greatly benefit your parish. I therefore propose to lay my propositions before you in confidence and in your Vicarage on Tuesday night, when I shall call upon you at midnight. There is no need to add that any treachery upon your part, which I do not look for, will be met with the direst reprisals against your Church and happiness. In any case you will listen to what I have to say if you are the sensible man I take you to be. —The Scarecrow.

When Doctor Syn unfolded his plan of dealing with this extraordinary situation, the General was so delighted that he detailed Major Faunce and a picked troop of Dragoons to put themselves under order of the Vicar of Dymchurch.

Thus it was that after the most careful preparation between Major Faunce, the Vicar and the sexton, Tuesday night at a quarter before twelve of the clock saw three men in the sheltered study of Doctor Syn. These three were the Vicar, the sexton and Craigen.

Now Craigen had for the last few days drunk himself into a glorious state of self-congratulation at the clever way in which he had hoodwinked judge and jury. But there was one thing which disturbed any feeling of security, and that was the mysterious disappearance of John's blood-stained suit.

In spite of his long spell of drinking since the inquiry, he remembered vividly that he had put it safely in the cupboard ceiling. Who then had taken it? It was in the hope of discovering this danger that had induced him to obey the Vicar's urgent request for him to visit him on that Tuesday night. Mipps had told him that his life was in danger, but that the good Vicar, whose province it was to look after the blackest sheep, was desirous of saving him. Thus it was that Craigen listened to the true version of his crimes, while Doctor Syn talked on with a pistol in his right hand and a gilt button in his left.

"I picked this up in the cabin of the Evenden boat," he said. "You deceived the Judge and jury, but not me, my friend. I recognized the button. I saw the three rings cut from the ladder, and God showed me what had happened. You dressed yourself in

John's clothes so that no blood should stain your own. You wait for Edmond in the darkness. As he falls you stab, knowing that John would be accused since you had spread the lie about their quarrel. Then your cunning plan miscarries. Hardly had you raised yourself from your first victim, but the next falls in upon you. John, rushing to the rescue, is also a victim of your knife, and while crouching over your second prey you conceive the thought of implicating the Scarecrow. Fool. The Scarecrow is a criminal who never makes mistakes. You do. You should have noticed this button. You should not have allowed me to give you Doctor Pepper's sleeping draught, for as soon as you were asleep I searched and found these." With his foot Doctor Syn lifted the lid of the iron chest and Craigen stared with horror at the blood-stained suit.

This discovery unnerved Craigen. "Hide them!" he whispered hoarsely.

Doctor Syn let the heavy lid fall back with a clang, and as if in echo there came a sharp knocking at the front door.

"See who it is, Mipps," ordered Syn.

Mipps returned with disquieting news for Craigen.

"It's a party of them Night-riders sent by the Scarecrow, Vicar. They wants to hang Craigen on the gallows in front of the Court House."

"Did you admit he was here?" asked Syn fearfully.

"No," replied Mipps. "But I said the Scarecrow was, and searching the house. He'll be coming out soon to search the stables, I says, and his orders is that you're to lie hid till Craigen appears."

"Why did you say that?" asked the Vicar.

"Because, sir," went on Mipps, "I remembered our old scarecrow in the turnip patch. Because I has also a dislike of seeing a man, even Craigen here, wriggling for life on our gallows. It's too near the churchyard where I works.

Because the garden being full of men waiting for Craigen, the only way he can get away to his boat is to dress in the scarecrow's rags." Craigen looked at Mipps in adoration, so that Doctor Syn, who had rehearsed Mipps in this very speech, was able to wink his amusement before adding: "Get the rags, then, while Craigen signs this confession of his crime.

And mark this, Craigen. If ever you return to this Marsh you shall hang." After dressing in the rags, Craigen signed and gladly accepted a purse of guineas to help him on his way. Then they let him out of the front door, closed it and waited. They heard his step on the gravel. A sharp word of command, and then a crackle of musketry. A fall, a rush of feet and then a knocking at the door. Mipps opened the door, and the Vicar walked out wearily. "Well?" he asked.

"The Scarecrow is dead," replied Major Faunce.

"And so would we have been if the Vicar hadn't given him a purse of guineas," said Mipps.

"Which I have great pleasure in restoring, reverend sir," replied the Major.

"May I add that you have played a brave part tonight in trapping this rascal for us."

"Are you quite sure he is dead?" asked Doctor Syn nervously.

"Be easy, sir," laughed the soldier. "I believe every shot went home. You may sleep soundly while we carry the body to Dover Castle to be hung in chains." But Doctor Syn did not sleep. No sooner had the Dragoons ridden away with Craigen's body stretched on an empty cannon carriage brought for the purpose, than the Vicar was riding on his pony towards the secret stable on the Marsh in which was kept the Scarecrow's horse Gehenna. Clad once more in his Scarecrow's rags, he turned to Mipps, who had preceded him, and said, "Come to me tomorrow and hear how the Dragoons witnessed the Scarecrow's resurrection." Then he galloped away towards Dover.

On the brow of the hill above Dover Town the Dragoons had halted, for a gust of wind had blown the sacking from the corpse. As they adjusted it a raucous voice cried out from the darkness: "You may kill my body but you'll never stop the Scarecrow's ghost from riding Romney Marsh. So to our next merry meeting, my valiant Dragoons." And then with a ringing of hoofs and diabolical yells the great black spectre of the Scarecrow thundered past them and vanished in the night.

Thus was the Scarecrow established as a ghost.

Chapter 18. The Bow Street Runner

Everybody realized that Doctor Syn, Vicar of Dymchurch, was the Scarecrow's chief enemy upon Romney Marsh. That both men were popular in their different ways went without saying, for while the Scarecrow led his merry rascals safely through many adventures, which if miscarrying would have meant the gallows, the rascals' pockets were well lined as a result, and their necks normal, so that since confidence in a man is the surest road to popularity, the Scarecrow was popular.

Also the very doubt as to whether the capable Captain of the Night-riders was a hero or devil, a man or a ghost, lent a mystery which is another part towards the laurels of popularity. Doctor Syn, on the other hand, was as fair and honest as the day. Everybody said that. None suspected that there was any mystery about him. If he did not talk much about his past—that was merely his unassuming way. A humility taught him not to talk about himself. This quality, in the days when the influential clergy were apt to be despotic, went a long way towards building up the popularity which he enjoyed; and though he would thunder against all forms of wickedness from the pulpit, he was ever tolerant with the sinner when he met him in the flesh.

Therefore his vigorous attacks against the Scarecrow and smuggling were perhaps to some surprising. They said that the Scarecrow was his dog-fish in the kiddle-net, which is fisherman's synonym for bee in the bonnet. He admitted the Scarecrow's ingenuity readily enough and expressed admiration for the man's daring. Everybody, in like manner, expressed their admiration for Doctor Syn's daring in ranging himself so deliberately against the Scarecrow; for it had been conclusively shown that anyone crossing swords with the Scarecrow came to disaster before long. Doctor Syn was constantly being warned by his well-wishers to leave the Scarecrow alone.

No doubt many of these advocates had their own good reasons for wishing the Scarecrow left alone, because he brought them very considerable gains. No doubt also but that some of them were genuinely afraid for the good Vicar, misguided though they thought him. For Doctor Syn made no secret when he was threatened, as he was repeatedly, by the Scarecrow himself. Whenever he received one or another of the Scarecrow's up-and-down scrawls of fearful warning, which were left in surprising places, such as under his pillow or upon his pulpit cushion, he would carry it to General Troubridge, who was for ever boasting that neither he nor Doctor Syn were to be intimidated by the ghostly rider, whatever other folk might be.

This was a sarcasm directed against Sir Antony Cobtree, who, although Leveller of the Marsh Scotts, Squire of Dymchurch, and Chief Magistrate upon the Marsh, preferred a pleasant life with his family, his horses, his dogs and tenants; and if a very generous allowance of the best brandy found its way mysteriously into his cellars—well, he was not the type of man to look a gift horse too closely in the mouth.

On the other hand, whenever Doctor Syn found a keg of brandy upon his Vicarage doorstep, with "Scarecrow's Compliments" scrawled in chalk upon it, he would send the same keg to the Customs officer, who, although drinking it himself, was nevertheless ready to swear in any company or court of inquiry that Doctor Syn's loyalty to the Government was clear. But for all this, Mipps the sexton would often make this remark to the Vicar when they were gone: "A keg to the Customs ain't wasted, sir. They enjoys a drink same as we does; and thank God we can produce as good brandy as any when we knows as how our guests are worthy of a good drink and to be trusted." It was surprising to many that despite Doctor Syn's continual outbursts against the Scarecrow, he viewed the nefarious exploits of Jimmie Bone the highwayman with extreme toleration. No one was more astonished at this attitude of the good Vicar than the famous Mr. Hunt the Bow Street Runner. He called at the Vicarage and presented his credentials.

"You're Doctor Syn, sir, Vicar of Dymchurch," he said, with the decision of a man who makes a statement and allows for no denial.

His tone amused the Vicar, who answered: "I have no reason to be ashamed of that, sir. I am also styled Dean of the Peculiars, which puts me on a pedestal a little above my colleagues hereabouts. Do you wish me to cry your name before the parish in holy matrimony, or what is it, Mr.—"

"Hunt, sir. An officer from Bow Street, at your service, I hope."

"As to that, Mr. Hunt," smiled Doctor Syn, "I cannot recall any deed of mine that can claim your service or professional attentions. Unless it is that you are a suitor for the hand of one of our pretty Marsh girls, and wish me to call the bans. Our fees are—"

"I ain't down here, sir," interrupted Hunt, "on any sentimental mission, I promise you. I ain't down here to put no banns up, but to slip the pretty darbies upon the wrists of Gentleman James, known, I believe, in these parts as Jimmie Bone."

"Mr. Hunt, you will admit that you are a stranger to me," replied the Vicar amiably. "There I deny your claim to expect me to ride with you against one of my most punctilious parishioners."

"Your what?" ejaculated Hunt.

"Please do not misunderstand me," went on the genial parson. "I do assure you that whenever I meet our notorious Jimmie, I do my best to make him see the error of his ways. But I must admit that there is no man under my ecclesiastical jurisdiction who is so punctilious in paying up his tithes in full. I take his word as to the figures he earns in sterling, and collect his tenth portion because it is my duty so to do. There is no canon that I know of which tells me that I must question the means of income. He tells me that he has earned so much, and I tell him that of that portion he owes the Church one tithe. Some people," continued the parson, "event amongst the gentry, make a fuss, Mr. Hunt, but Mr. Bone, never. Now you may or you may not have heard of another outlaw of these parts. He is called the Scarecrow. Had you been sent from Bow Street to arrest him, you would have found me a worthy and not unhelpful ally.

The Scarecrow certainly enriches our part of the world in his mysterious way, but he does not pay his tithes as our romantic gentleman of the road does. By the way, Mr. Bone lives up to his ancient profession fully. I never yet heard that he has ever robbed a poorer than himself. The rich, yes, but the poor never, and when he robs the rich, it is not only my fund for the Sick and Needy that benefits, but I hear many of the poorest of the Marsh as well have full cause to bless his skill, his generosity and luck."

"And a very long speech, too, sir, in defence of this gentleman of the road," replied Hunt. "Every man to his own calling and to what advantage he can gain from it. But let me point out that this Bone fellow has a reward upon his head.

He may do as much filching from your local gentry bumpkins as he pleases for all I care, but, you see, he has repeatedly robbed His Majesty's mails, and His Majesty's Justices in London have employed Jerry Hunt, at your service, to carry their justice for them into this fifth quarter of the globe, for I believe your arrogant Marshmen lay claim to that title?"

"Quite so, sir, and with full justice," returned Doctor Syn. "Our schools upon the Marsh teach our children here this formula in geography—that the world is divided into five parts: Europe, Asia, Africa, the Americas and Romney Marsh. Aye, sir, and you will find that we are the most independent of them all. By giving us our independence during a troublous age, King William secured a certain good loyalty for his successors. Therefore I defend Mr. Bone, and not the Scarecrow, for you see one pays his tithes and the other does not.

But if you are in the Bow Street business for your income, why not abandon the meagre two hundred pounds which is set upon the head of the highwayman and try to earn the two thousand guineas that are set upon the capture, dead or alive, of the great smuggler?"

"I have a mind to get both of them in one journey," laughed the Bow Street runner. "And if it so be that you can help me to one or either, well then, reverend sir, I promise that your tithes shall not be at a loss for me."

"I will do all I can to help you catch the Scarecrow," replied Syn, "but I am powerless to aid you against Mr. Bone. I will, however, do one thing for you. I will save you time, and Bow Street your longer billeting expense. Mr. Bone held up the mails the other day, and when he paid his tithes to me in confidence, an of course under an assumed name, I gathered that the chase was hot upon his spurs, and that it was more than likely that your chief, Sir John Fielding of Bow Street, would be sending the famous Mr. Hunt upon his trail.

He quite realized that, when one constantly was in the habit of holding up the King's mail, ere long Mr. Hunt would be put upon his track. And he was right," Syn went on, "for here you are, Mr. Hunt, and Gentleman James is by this time, I should imagine, quietly enjoying a tour of the Picardy churches. You may not know it, but not the least of his many good qualities is a very intelligent appreciation of ecclesiastical architecture. I advised this present tour myself. He had not seen the beauties of Picardy. It is a great pity in some ways that Mr. Bone should be a highwayman, for he would make an excellent Dean's Verger of Canterbury Cathedral."

"So you mean to tell me that the party I'm looking for has gone to France?" asked Hunt, with a frown of annoyance.

"I did not exactly tell you so," replied Doctor Syn humbly. "I just said that I imagined so. Oh, and by the way, Mr. Hunt," he went on amiably, "it is no use looking at me in such a very antagonistic manner. You see, I am a parson, and a parson is one who is perhaps even more at the beck and call of the sinner than the saint. Lost sheep, and all that, you know. Besides, I confess that I rather like Mr. Bone. I only wish I could say the same of this rascally Scarecrow. Now come, Mr. Hunt, why not—as indeed you must, unless, of course, it happens that you are too interested in Picardy churches—why not, I say, join with me in hounding out and down this other outlaw, the Scarecrow? What the Customs, the Navy and the Dragoons have failed to do, Mr. Hunt of Bow Street might accomplish. I'll help you in that quest, and when you get the reward—well, I confess, although I want nothing for myself, I will gladly accept what you care to give for my Sick and Needy Fund. In fact, Mr. Hunt, against the highwayman you will find me as close as an oyster, but against this rascally non-paying tithe man, the Scarecrow, I will give you what help I can and be as open as your own red waistcoat."

"How can you help me?" asked Hunt.

"In the first place by advice," replied Doctor Syn. "Take off that absurd red waistcoat and try not to look so confoundedly like what you are. The folk in this part of the globe are not fond of foreigners, so behave pleasantly, spend money freely, and make a good pretence of your inferiority to any Marshman. Above all, follow my instructions implicitly. I may tell you—indeed anyone will tell you—that I have twice delivered the Scarecrow into the hands of the authorities, but they have allowed him to escape through not taking the full measure of his ingenuity."

"He'll not escape Jerry Hunt," laughed the man from Bow Street.

"But you must understand this," went on the Vicar. "I will not be questioned by you or any of your legal friends as to how I come by my information. If I tell you, for instance, that there is to be a big run of contraband next week, on Wednesday night to be exact, and that the Scarecrow will direct it, you must not say to me, 'How come you by that knowledge, and from whom?' Because you see, Mr. Hunt, that is a sore point which very often pricks my conscience. I visit the sick, and who talks so much as the sick, eh? There you have it. I pick up unconsidered trifles of gossip, and then piece them together."

"Jerry Hunt puts himself entirely at your service, Doctor Syn. What is more, I'll take off my red waistcoat and leave it here with you till I return to Bow Street with the darbies on the Scarecrow."

"The darbies on the Scarecrow," repeated Doctor Syn. "What an inspired sentence, Mr. Hunt! I only wonder whether it will come true."

"I'll trust you for orders, and you trust Jerry Hunt for results," replied the other, divesting himself of his waistcoat before taking up his quarters at the Ship Inn, where he endeavoured to look as much like an ordinary traveller as possible. But for all that he was conscious of being watched, and found that the natives were more than suspicious. This was no doubt due to Doctor Syn, who had immediately passed the word to Sexton Mipps that the visitor was none other than the great Bow Street Runner. A warning was also sent to Jimmie Bone that Hunt was after him, but that Doctor Syn had drawn a red herring across his path.

This was on the Saturday; and at night, behind closed shutters at the Vicarage, Doctor Syn, Mipps and Jimmie Bone met in consultation. Doctor Syn did most of the talking. The other two listened and nodded, though often protesting against the daring of the scheme which the Vicar unfolded. But the Vicar would rule them down with "It cannot miscarry, because I shall depend as much upon you two as upon myself, and you will not fail me, any more than I could fail you." So these two men, the sexton and the highwayman, the only men in England who were in a position to identify Syn as the Scarecrow, these two trusted lieutenants lifted their glasses and drank to the Doctor's scheme. This was on Saturday night.

It was on Sunday morning that the blow fell, which made the village almost forget the presence of Hunt the Runner, though the news of his arrival had been discussed in every tavern from Hythe to Lydd. Hunt had no idea how speedily dangerous news could spread on Romney Marsh.

The blow fell in church at Morning Prayer. The bells had rung. They had stopped when the Cobtree family had assembled in the Squire's pew. General Troubridge was with them, in order to hear Doctor Syn preach. Now the bells always stopped when the Squire rose from his knees and looked over the pew side through his quizzing glass, in order to see who was there and who was not.

The stopping of the bells at the right moment was supposed to deceive the parish that the Squire was always punctual. It was also a signal for Doctor Syn to intone a blessing upon the choir and service from the vestry. Upon this Sunday, however, his voice was not heard. The silence developed into an awkward pause.

Mipps beckoned to the beadle, and the Squire beckoned to Mipps, and eventually the beadle was sent trotting to the Vicarage to see what had delayed the Vicar. But the Vicar was not at the Vicarage. Mrs. Fowey, the housekeeper, to whom the beadle whispered over her pew, thought that the Vicar had gone out after breakfast. The Squire ordered the choir to take their places and sing a hymn. But still there was no Vicar. The Squire announced to the congregation that no doubt the Vicar had been detained at the cottage of some dying parishioner, and to eke out the time he stood up at the desk and read a warlike chapter from Joshua. Still no Vicar. As he closed the great Bible, preparatory to dismissing the congregation, he saw for the first time a paper lying on the desk cushion. He read it silently and then gasped aloud. There were some who maintained that he swore aloud. He then decided to read the message publicly.

"Doctor Syn would take no Warning. He was becoming a Menace to me and to the Safety of the Night-riders. So I have been compelled to carry out my Threat. I have removed the Vicar of Dymchurch.

"(Signed) The Scarecrow."

After urging every able-bodied man to search and rescue the good Vicar, he dismissed the Service.

Now, much to the astonishment of Mr. Hunt, who had attended church out of respect for his secret ally, Doctor Syn, the Squire tapped him on the shoulder in the churchyard, and requested him, by name, to accompany him to the Court House.

Here, after promising not only to discover Doctor Syn, but also to arrest the Scarecrow, he asked Sir Antony how he had known him for Hunt the Runner.

"We are not entirely ignorant down here, sir, of our London," replied the Squire. "Indeed, some of us cut a pretty good figure there in the best society.

Hence I for one immediately recognized Hunt of Bow Street." Hunt was both flattered and hurt. Flattered that he was known; hurt that he had been so easily unmasked against his wish.

To the General's offer of military help he turned a deaf ear. Hunt had no wish to share with others the large reward that had been set upon the Scarecrow's head, and so he assured the gentlemen that only by being given a free and lone hand could he hope to effect his capture. "But leave me alone, gentlemen, and I'll soon have the darbies upon your Scarecrow's wrists, and furthermore, if Doctor Syn ain't dead he'll be in his pulpit next sabbath apreaching a very interesting sermon, I have no doubt." There was no news, however, all through that Sunday, and Monday produced no results. Mipps went about sad and morose. Tuesday—nothing.

Mrs. Fowey went about moaning loudly. Even the folk who most admired the Scarecrow and profited by his cargoes thought he had gone too far in thus kidnapping the Vicar.

The news of the Wednesday "run" being generally known, the Squire agreed that in spite of Hunt's request, at least one troop of the Dragoons should be in residence. Hearing of this, Hunt laid his own plans without consultation with the Squire. Confident that Wednesday night would bring the Scarecrow out upon the Marsh, he determined to get a sight of him. For it happened that a wild and fantastic idea had entered into Hunt's brain, which had to be proved or disproved before he could act upon it.

On Wednesday evening he retired to his room, saying that the Marsh drinks were too strong for a mere Londoner, and that his head was throbbing. He was neither surprised nor annoyed to find that his door had been secured from the outside and that he was a supposed prisoner. He had planned to go by the casement in any case, and for that purpose had provided himself with a strong length of cord. Thus it was that by eleven o'clock he was sweeping Dymchurch beach and bay through a spy-glass, and lying comfortably hidden on the top of a haystack in the centre of the Marsh.

He had heard much talk in London about the Scarecrow and his Night-riders of Romney Marsh, but he had never imagined that the organization was run on such a big scale, and this particular run was an important landing, with a full fleet of luggers in commission. First he saw flash signals playing like will-o'- the-wisps all over the Marsh. Then a great beacon was fired from Aldington Knoll, and on the full tide he saw many vessels, lighted up by the full moon, putting into the bay in perfect formation.

But the smugglers were not to have it all their own way. He heard the ring of hoofs upon the Marsh round beneath him. A sharp word of command. The sound of trotting broke into a canter coming nearer; and then there swept by a troop of Dragoons with drawn sabres, and the moonlight dancing on their bright helmets.

As he watched them disappear, the bright flash and sharp bark of a gun made him swing his spy-glass to the sea. A fast vessel under full sail, and firing as she raced, came skimming through the water towards the smuggling fleet. It was, as Hunt knew, the Revenue cutter from Sandgate. Her gallant fire was immediately answered by the five ships that flanked the smuggling fleet upon the starboard side, and while the luggers and fishing boats held on their course towards the beach, these five tacked round to meet the cutter, who, seeing herself outnumbered and outgunned, swung round and stood for home, closely followed by the smugglers' fighting ships.

As Hunt was cursing the inadequate Customs' defence, he suddenly saw a tall wild figure, mounted on a fierce black horse, silhouetted against the skyline about a hundred yards away. It was the Scarecrow. Raising one arm above his head, he fired a pistol to the sky, which was answered by a wild yell, as from the back of the farm buildings behind Hunt's haystack a mad cavalcade of ghastly mounted devils swept out across the road and, leaping the dykes with screams of derision, galloped across country towards the flank of the Dragoons, who were borne away and scattered by the out-numbering Night-riders.

Hunt saw the Dragoons scattered and driven off with the same ease as the Revenue cutter had been herded back to Dover harbour, and the mad Nightriders galloped off towards the beach, where a long string of pack ponies was 262_ __being loaded up with tubs and bales. The Scarecrow's organization had once more shown itself superior to the inefficiency of the authorities. "And serve them right," muttered Hunt to himself as he dropped to the ground, with the brave hope of now catching the Scarecrow single-handed.

Once again the Scarecrow was victorious. Astride his great horse, and surrounded by his Night-riders, he received his gallopers: messengers who brought news that the various sections of pack ponies had reached the hills and deposited their goods in the "hides" before scattering for home and stables. The last to gallop was Hellspite, who had only to announce "All clear, Scarecrow," for the Night-riders also to be dismissed. Before he could speak, the Scarecrow rasped out, "Were any of our men hurt in the skirmish with those damned Dragoons?"

"Aye, Scarecrow," replied the little devil. "One or two lads with gashes who gave as good as they got. But I've a message that there's a man a-dyin' at Black's Farm. He offered his purse of guineas to any messenger who could fetch our prisoner, Parson Syn. A religious cove, Scarecrow; for he said, 'Ask the Scarecrow in the name of God and fair play to let the parson come quick, so that I can die repentant.' He crept to Black's to die. Mother Black let him in, as her old 'un's with the lads at Aldington. A dreadful gash. He looks like a goner to me."

"Do you know him?" asked the Scarecrow, motioning Hellspite to ride with him out of earshot.

Hellspite shook his masked head. "His face was tied up to stop the blood and I couldn't get nothin' out of him but 'Fetch the parson for a prayer.'" The Scarecrow leant down from his saddle and whispered in the little man's ear: "Mipps, we must go there. I'll not have a man die uncomforted. Doctor Syn must be there."

Mipps began protesting, but the Scarecrow cut him short with: "A dying man, Mipps. The parson must sometimes come before the adventurer." Riding back towards his devil-masked followers, he ordered: "Come. I have business at Black's Farm. You will await me there for orders." A quarter of an hour's hard riding brought them to the farm. The Scarecrow, Hellspite and a tall devil called Beelzebub, after tying their horses to the fence, were admitted to the house. After a gruff word of thanks to Mother Black for harbouring the wounded man, the Scarecrow ordered her to her bed, while Mipps led him to the room.

"This is the powder closet," whispered Mipps, "and very convenient too. He lies through that door. Shall I get his candle?"

"I will," replied the Scarecrow. "Wait here. Beelzebub, guard the passage door."

Through one of the folds of the blood-soaked bandage the dying man saw the ghastly mask of the Scarecrow surveying him in the moonlight.

"I have sent for the parson," said the rough, harsh voice.

The dying man began to mutter his thanks, but the other cut him short with:

"Don't thank me. I've no love for parsons. Don't believe in 'em. But if a dying man asked for my last drop of brandy I'd give it up." Another voice came from the powder closet. "They've brought the old parson, Scarecrow. Shall he come up?"

"I'll come," replied the Scarecrow, carrying the candle with him.

Sheltered by the half-closed door, and assisted by Mipps and the candlelight in the mirror, he quickly and silently stripped off the mask and rags, beneath which appeared the black clerical suit of Doctor Syn. From a side pocket he shook out the parson's formal wig. During which operation he addressed himself for the benefit of the dying man in the Scarecrow's voice.

"He's in there, Parson Syn. Deceive the poor devil that he's safe for heaven if you can, and maybe we'll forgo a little of your punishment. But no tricks, mind, and not too long with your prayer."

"I will do what I can for him," replied the sweet calm voice of Doctor Syn.

As he took a last look at himself in the mirror, Mipps saw his master give a sudden start. Although the little sexton did not understand the reason for alarm, he understood the silent signal which followed, for Doctor Syn pointed sharply to the floor, and then made a crawling gesture with his long fingers. Like a well-trained dog, Mipps dropped quietly on his stomach as his master, shielding the flame with his hand, tiptoed into the room.

"Is that Doctor Syn?" whispered the wounded man.

"Aye, come to pray with you, my poor fellow," replied the parson. "But ere I begin, if you can bethink you of any crime upon your soul, now is the time to confess it."

"There is one thing," said the dying man. "But whether you will think it a crime or not I cannot say."

"Let me be the judge of it, then," replied the parson.

"Well, sir, is it a crime to act the spy in order to send the cleverest rogue unhung to the gallows?" Doctor Syn sat by the bed considering this before replying: "Good men have from time to time been forced to play the spy. The spies of Joshua were accounted good men and brave. But you must tell me more."

"I will, sir," whispered back the dying man, putting his left hand with a great effort up to his wounded head as though the pain were too much to bear.

Then with one superb gesture, which peeled the blood-stained bandage from his head and flung the bedclothes back, the dying man was sitting up on the bed, and Doctor Syn found himself looking into the barrel of a pistol held by the Bow Street Runner.

That Doctor Syn was amazed appeared only too plainly to the grinning Hunt.

"I told the Squire I'd find Doctor Syn. I have; and found him out as well. I told you I'd put the darbies on the Scarecrow too. Very clever, Doctor Scarecrow, but Jerry Hunt's been a bit cleverer. If the spies of Joshua is accounted good 'uns, what will they say of Jerry Hunt now? No offence, Mr. Parson Smuggler, but out with your wrists and we'll have the darbies on." Doctor Syn did not move. He blinked at the pistol, and then shook his head sadly. "Mr. Hunt," he said quietly, "you are a brave man, but a very foolish one. I will not discuss the absurdity of your statement here. It is too laughable, and our present situation is too serious. I have suffered so much in the last few days at the hands of this rascally

Scarecrow that I assure you I welcome your presence here with all my heart. You are at least brave, strong and ingenious, and if you can get me away from these ghastly Night-riders, even with the darbies on my wrists, I will forgive your ridiculous accusation."

"I'll get you away—don't worry," chuckled Hunt. "There's a great manure heap under this window. A bit dirty for a parson, but it will break our fall together in silence. And you shall have a wash before facing the magistrate, I promise you."

"And I promise you that if you don't drop that pistol you're deader than your manure heap. Sharp's the word." And sharp it was; for Mr. Hunt felt cold steel pricking steadily into his shirted back. Hunt lowered his pistol and turned to see the owner of the cold words and steel, and in that second Doctor Syn struck hard at his wrist. The pistol dropped. "We'll have no murder, Mr. Hunt," he said, "Night-riders or no."

"Give me that pistol, Parson Syn," ordered Hellspite, pressing the dagger bayonet of his blunderbuss against the Runner's back. Yes, Mipps had understood his master's gesture, and had crawled behind the bed when Doctor Syn had entered. With pistol and blunderbuss he now had the whip hand.

"Now, Parson," he ordered, "save your skin by fetching in the Scarecrow. He's outside." Doctor Syn, with a gesture of resignation, went out, and a few moments later the Scarecrow and Beelzebub came in with ropes. They bound Mr. Hunt securely, and gagged his mouth with blood-stained bandages.

"Since he prefers the window, let him go by it," laughed the Scarecrow.

Prodded by the blunderbuss bayonet, Hunt was pricked to the casement, hoisted up, and dropped on to the manure, where he was pounced upon by the waiting Night-riders. Thrown over the Scarecrow's saddle, the whole cavalcade set off at the trot for Dymchurch. They halted at the twin-posted gallows between the Court House and the churchyard wall. Hunt gave up all hope when he saw that emblem of justice, the hanging noose. He was agreeably surprised when at the Scarecrow's orders he was but lashed securely to the right-hand post.

"And now, lads," croaked the Scarecrow, "home to bed and dream of the guineas you have earned tonight." The Night-riders wheeled their horses and rode off in different directions to their homes. From the crowd of some seventy horsemen only three remained:Hellspite, who still held Hunt's pistol, but pointing towards a tall Night-rider whom they had called Beelzebub, and the

Scarecrow. Hunt fell to wondering what the Night-rider had done to be thus guarded. He was soon undeceived.

"Off with our uniform, Hellspite," ordered the Scarecrow, "and lash the meddlesome parson to the left-hand post." The Night-rider dismounted, and at the point of the pistol took off his rags and mask, and the astonished Hunt saw them bind a very weary Doctor Syn to the fellow post. Then Hellspite climbed the post and nailed two papers above their heads.

"'Scarecrow's warning' is what the papers say," explained the Scarecrow.

"If so be that anyone cuts you free in the morning, you will, I know, have learnt your lesson, Doctor Syn, for you are no fool. In future keep to your preaching and leave honest men alone. As to you, Hunt, let me warn you, if you or any other of your Bow Street trash set foot upon our Marsh again, it will not be lashing but hanging to this gallows you an look for. So let us hope for your own sake that you will be freed in time to catch the morning coach. Good night."

By dawn Hunt had worked his gag sufficiently loose to be able to talk to his companion in misfortune.

"I thought so," said Doctor Syn kindly. "You see, I saw you sitting up in bed and watching me change in the mirror. Naturally you thought I must be the Scarecrow, because you did not know that these rascals have kept me dressed in their infernal rags since first they took me. He's a cunning rogue, this Scarecrow. Did you note that he dismissed his men before lashing me up? No doubt he thought that many of them would not agree to violence against me.

You see, I am not entirely unpopular even amongst the rogues of the parish." Hunt realized then that even a Bow Street Runner might be guilty of a bad mistake, and was generous enough to own as much to Doctor Syn, and to ask his pardon, which the Vicar gladly gave.

They remained there talking till the morning broke. The village being strangely sleepy, the first person to notice their plight was the Squire himself, who stepped out for a breath of air before his breakfast.

Thought the good Vicar seemed badly shaken after his mysterious adventures, he refused to say a word, affirming that he had promised if released to stay silent, and so must keep his word. At to Hunt, although he promised to call upon the Squire when he had cleaned himself at the inn he was so fearful of losing the coach that he did not trouble even to call at the Vicarage for his read waistcoat. He went post haste to London, where he kept his mouth shut, not caring to boast of his misfortunes on Romney Marsh.

That night Gentleman James tapped upon the closed shutters of the Vicarage study about midnight, and was admitted to the Vicar by the sexton.

"Ah, my good Jimmie Bone," said Doctor Syn. "You have come to be congratulated, I presume, upon your excellent imitation of the Scarecrow. It was vastly entertaining to me and very bewildering to Hunt. Have some brandy."

"I really came to pay tithes," grinned the highwayman, removing his silk mask. "Just held up another coach. A hundred guineas in all. That means ten to you."

"The Parish Accounts, please, Mipps," said the Vicar, taking the coins. "I suppose it is useless for me to point out to you, James, the error of your ways?"

"Quite," replied the highwayman, drinking.

"Pity, perhaps," said Doctor Syn, entering ten guineas in the columns of the Sick and Needy Fund. "But you are a good fellow, Jimmie. At least you pay your tithes."

Chapter 19. The press-gang pressed

Although General Troubridge invariably quarrelled with his twin brother, Admiral Troubridge, there was one subject on which they not only agreed but actually co-operated in support of it. The subject which brought these cantankerous old warriors into unity was the Press-gang. Needless to say, very few people agreed with them, for the general opinion was that the Pressgang was an odious and barbaric institution, detrimental to the freedom of the citizen. To this, however, the Troubridges would reply: "The only way to maintain the freedom of the citizen is to keep His Majesty's Forces up to strength. If men will not join the Colours of their own will, then the Press-gang is the only solution." On a cold but bright November morning a party of this "odious institution", consisting of nine picked men under the command of a petty-officer named Stubbard, came swinging along the main road from Dover. Chosen carefully for this particular job, they were about as rough a crowd as could be found in the King's Navy, and altogether presented a very formidable appearance. Weatherbeaten hulks every man of them, their faces tanned to a deep mahogany, and their muscles as hard as iron. In addition to their cutlasses they carried their kit bundles slung on to stout oak cudgels.There was no pretence at any secrecy, for on each side of the gigantic Stubbard marched two little powder monkeys, one boy proudly banging away at a deep side drum, while the other led the sailors' whistling tunes on a long fife.

Not an able-bodied man did they encounter from Dover to Sandgate, for at the sound of their arrogant music, their likely victims made themselves uncommonly scarce. But this did not trouble Stubbard. He was on a special commission, bound for distant Dymchurch.

"Stubbard," the Admiral had said to him, "the best manhood in this country of Kent is to be found on Romney Marsh. That damned Scarecrow picks his men well, and knocks 'em into fine shape too. If a man is strong enough to carry tubs against the Government, he's strong enough to carry cannon-balls against the foreigner. Go and collect as many of the rascals as you can, and send them in irons aboard the Revenue cutter. I need not tell you that if you can include the Scarecrow himself in one of your batches, the better I'll be pleased.

My brother the General has put a big price on the rascal's head, and that, added to the Government reward, would set you and your lads up very well in prizemoney. But you must use brains as well as your muscles, for this Scarecrow is about as mighty as a sperm whale, and if he finds you robbing young bulls from his school, you may look out for white water." Stubbard had heard much talk about the Phantom Rider of Romney Marsh, but unlike his breed he was not superstitious, and he felt confident that could he but get within striking distance of the Scarecrow, one scientific blow with a belaying-pin would put an end to any more of the ridiculous ghost stories that were circulating.

Stubbard broke the march at Sandgate to allow his men a meal of fried fish at a wooden shanty upon the water-front. The proprietor obligingly sent his boy out for grog, and through the convivial conversation that followed he learned that the hated Press-gang were bound for Dymchurch. But the proprietor was a closer man with his tongue than the boastful Stubbard, who never dreamed that he was talking to one of the Scarecrow's most trusted agents. Indeed, so trusty was he that no sooner were the Press-gang out of sight from his shop window, and once more upon the march, than the dealer in fried fish was saddling up his horse.

Knowing that the sailors would keep to the sea-road, he climbed the hill, and by galloping around the summit was able to ride down into Hythe High Street ahead of them. He then rode hard for Dymchurch, and was fortunate in finding Sexton Mipps at work in the churchyard. They had plenty of time to call in at the taverns and pass the word that the Press-gang were on the way. Drinks were hurriedly swallowed, and by the time the drum and fife were heard from the sea-wall the male population of Dymchurch were nowhere to be seen.

Stubbard, who was well provided with Admiralty cash, repaired to the Ship Inn to command billeting for his men, and in spite of Mrs. Waggetts' protestations that she was a lone widow and could not deal with ten ruffianly men in her establishment, Stubbard overruled her and took possession, paying a day's board in advance. Asking whether the inn was the best frequented in the village, Stubbard learned that there was very little custom at any of the local taverns, as the Dymchurch men were either too old to go gadding about drinking, or too young to have learned the taste for strong waters. "Indeed," said the landlady, "if you have come to collect men for the Colours, you will find Dymchurch an unlucky place for your purpose. Do you suppose for one moment that I would be a widow for the last two years if there were any ablebodied men about the place?" Stubbard thought it more than likely, but held his peace.

"Wait till the sun sets, lads," he laughed to his men, "and we'll see the manhood of Dymchurch crowding into the taverns for their drinks." But in this Stubbard was doomed to disappointment, for that night saw three taverns with empty bars. Not a man of serviceable age was to be seen.

Exception must be made, however, for Mr. Mipps. All the Press-gangs of England would not have kept him out of an inn when he wanted a drink.

But it was not the usually quick-moving Mipps that went there. No, Mipps was not above taking precautions. A useful man on a man-o'-war was a carpenter, especially one who had most of his life been a ship's carpenter, and sailed over the seven seas. He had no wish to transfer from the Night-riders to the Navy, so he walked slowly, with his toes turned in, and dragging one leg in a limp. Likewise, he hunched up one shoulder as high as it would lift, and carried his head on one side. He went even so far as to tell the sea-dogs that he took it as a great insult that no Press-gang had ever compelled his services.

"But where are the young men of the place, my jolly old sexton?" asked Stubbard.

Mipps went to the casement and pointed towards the churchyard.

"There they lie, what there was of 'em, mister," replied the little man. "All as dead as mutton. Folk around here are either born old or die young. Most unhealthy spot this, what with marsh fever and worse."

"And what's worse than the fever, eh?" asked Stubbard.

Mipps made a very good attempt at a shudder as he whispered: "Them things what rides on the Marsh. Phantom horsemen, my son. It's death to meet 'em. Aye, and don't you laugh neither, my brave boys, I've seen 'em, and come off luckier than most. I wasn't always bent and twisted as you see me now. You see, like a fool I went out on the Marsh one night where no one of sense ought to go, and I meets the Scarecrow hisself on his spectral horse. I was glad enough to go home with no more than a bad twistin'. He just looks at me fiercelike, and I felt myself go all blarsted. Stricken like a tree with lightning." Although they laughed at the old man's fancies, they did not feel quite so comfortable when they looked out over the great lonely Marsh.

Stubbard waited till nightfall in the Ship Inn, but not a man came in for a drink except the sexton, so falling in his men he went round to the other two taverns which the village boasted. But there again he found empty bars.

Returning to the Ship and cursing the village for its temperance, he surprised Mrs. Waggetts clearing a goodly row of wet tankards from the bar.

"So the rats have been in for drinks behind our backs, eh?" he said.

The landlady lied, assuring him that she had only left the sailors' tankards there for the sake of company.

"Very convenient to have two doors to a bar like you've got," replied Stubbard sarcastically. "Well, we'll be biding here till the cunning rats show themselves. The Navy wants them to fight the French and the Americans, and by thunder if she can't get 'em by fair means we'll get 'em for her by foul." The next day Stubbard paraded his men up and down the village street, while the powder-monkeys tried their best to bring the place to life with music; for by this means Stubbard hoped to attract the children, so that he could question them about their big brothers, fathers and uncles. But not a child answered the call of curiosity. The Vicar had ordered a special holiday so that they could not be waylaid on their journey to school.

"Well, it's the Sabbath tomorrow, lads," said Stubbard. "We'll fill a pew for once, and keep our eyes open for likely men during the sermon. Folk what are so temperate over drinks will not resist going to church, I'm thinking." But again Stubbard was to be disappointed, for the congregation consisted entirely of women and children, and the only presentable man was the Squire himself, and he was too exalted a gentleman for the Press-gang to play any tricks with, although Stubbard was all but driven to hit him on the head when he had the effrontery to wait for them in the churchyard and congratulate him for having brought such a good muster to the service.

Doctor Syn, the Vicar, was also pleased to be gracious, telling Stubbard that it was indeed a great pleasure to him to see such fine fellows in his church.

Stubbard found his men were none too pleased with their experience. They grumbled at having been ordered to church for nothing. However, Stubbard issued extra grog allowance, and promised that if no likely men appeared soon, he would break in and search every house in the village. "And God help the first man we catch," he said. "We'll show them that we are not to be laughed at." That very night they gained their first victim in a manner that set the whole village afire with indignation.

Young Hadley's wife was ill, and he had to risk the lurking Press-gang in order to get to the doctor. The front garden of Sennacherib Pepper's residence was a good lurking-place by reason of the cover of garden wall and trees.

Hadley was striding towards the physician's front door when the gang surrounded him with their cudgels. They carried him away to the sea-wall, and flashed a signal to the Revenue cutter which was anchored in the bay. A boat came ashore and the unconscious young husband was thrown in, and in the morning discovered that he was in irons and in the hold. He raved and swore to no avail, crying out that this would be the death of his wife.

When the news of this outrage became known, Hadley's two brothers and father went to the Squire and lodged a protest. Sir Antony Cobtree promised to do all he could, though, knowing Admiral Troubridge supported the Press-gang, he said frankly that he could not hold out much hope of Hadley being released.

This enraged the Hadleys and they went to the Ship Inn, with their tempers strung to murder point. But they were no match for the Press-gang, who served them the same as their young relative, while Stubbard chuckled to himself to think what fools they had been to rush into the trap. Mipps had been a witness when they knocked the Hadleys out, and he carried the news to Doctor Syn.

On receiving certain instructions from the Vicar, Mipps went back to the inn, where he pretended to get talkative over his drink. Stubbard not only listened to what he had to say, but encouraged him to talk more, and when at last Mipps staggered out for his bed, Stubbard's triumph was complete.

"I've pumped that little sexton dry, lads," he confided to his men. "There's to be a 'run' tomorrow night, and this Scarecrow is to direct it, and the sexton assures me that if we hide at a place called Black's Farm we'll see the Scarecrow and his Phantom Riders. Now if we can get the Scarecrow, well and good, and we're all made men, but in any case we'll get some of them. Our tack is to watch out for stragglers, twos or threes, and bowl 'em out." But the next night was destined to hold some surprises for Stubbard and his gang, and for the Admiral too, as things fell out.

During the day, Stubbard and his men went out to Black's

Farm and took careful note of the ground. There seemed to be no one there to interfere with them, so they caught four fowls from the farmyard and roasted them over a gipsy fire, while Stubbard unfolded his plans in a loud voice, every word of which was overheard by the farmhands, who were safely hidden in a smugglers' room in the roof.

After washing down their stolen dinner with some brandy which they discovered in the abandoned kitchen, Stubbard marched them back to get some sleep at the Ship Inn, telling the powder-monkeys to wake them at eight o'clock. Though longing for sleep themselves, the poor boys did not dare to close their eyes for fear of failing in their duty. All they hoped for was that Stubbard might leave them behind so that they could sleep till their lords and masters returned from their night's adventure.

But that was not Stubbard's way. There would be rough and tumble, and the more heads they saw cracked in their youth, the more useful would they be to the Navy in their manhood. They were merely told to leave the drum and the fife behind, as there must be no noise, and also that they could then carry the grog tub. By nine o'clock the party were safely entrenched in a dry dyke that was within a stone's throw of Black's Farm.

They had a long and dreary wait, enlivened about midnight by gunfire at sea. It was the Revenue cutter attacking the smugglers' fleet. Three of the luggers replied to the fire with spirit, but the Press-gang could not see the results, for all vessels were suddenly swallowed up in the sea mist.

"If that sexton has hoodwinked me about this spot, I'm sorry for him," growled Stubbard. "No signs of those phantoms yet he talked about."

"Not phantoms, but men: smugglers," whispered one of the gang.

True enough, they heard voices, and a minute later saw a party of three men cross a foot-bridge and enter the same field.

"Come on, lads, we'll make sure of these at any rate," whispered Stubbard.

"They're strong-looking, and will be good prizes. Come."

Out of the dyke they scrambled with cudgels in hand and their cutlasses loosened in the scabbards. As it happened, one of the powder-monkeys was actually the quickest to get over the lip of the dyke, and thus finding himself for a second alone in advance he turned to see whether the others were following him. As he turned he let out the most ghastly scream of terror, so much so that the sailors forgot the smugglers for the moment and turned to see what the lad was pointing at. It was the Phantom Horseman. The Scarecrow himself. There he sat grinning at them upon his gigantic black horse, not twenty yards behind them. So that there should be no doubt as to his identity, he cried out in mocking, raucous voice: "Yes, I am the Scarecrow. Are you going to take me? Am not I a fine figure for your Horse Marines?" To do Stubbard justice, he was the first to recover, and waving his cutlass above his head, he shouted to his men: "There's prize-money to last us a lifetime. Follow me."

Bravely he jumped back into the dry dyke and clambered up the other side before his men could move from their astonishment.

The Scarecrow drew a pistol from his holster and cried out, "Stay where you are." Stubbard replied: "Shoot and be damned to you. I ain't afraid."

"You will be," croaked the Scarecrow, reining his horse back on to his haunches, so that he pawed the air with his terrible fore-hoofs. But instead of firing straight as Stubbard expected, the Phantom Horseman fired above his head, and at that signal the most dreadful howl arose, as round from the back of Black's Farm some fifty Night-riders came galloping. The sight of their hideous masks, their wild blazing cloaks, and fierce bare-backed horses demoralized the sailors, who were fighting out of their element. The cutlasses and short cudgels were useless against the longs stout poles which the riders used as lances.

Outnumbered, they were ridden down beneath the weight of the fierce charge.

Afraid of the horses' hoofs, they huddled on the ground without striking a blow.

All save the desperate Stubbard. He aimed a swinging blow at the Scarecrow's horse, but the rider took it on his long blade, and with a twisting wrench ripped the cutlass from the sailor's hand and dug his point deep into his forearm.

"The Press-gang pressed," laughed the Scarecrow. "The Hadleys are avenged. Now let's see whether these poor lands have the strength to carry tubs." With the precision of trained cavalry, half the troop dismounted, and while some of them covered the sailors at pistol point, others bound their arms to their sides with cords prepared for the purpose. These had been cut long enough to allow a rider to grasp the end.

"What about these boys, Scarecrow?" asked one of the smugglers who grasped the terrified powder-monkeys by the wrists.

"Poor little devils," rasped the Scarecrow. "Shame on you, Mr. Stubbard, to bring such youngsters out on dirty work. Well, they shall have a joy-ride: aye, an adventure that will make you the envy of all the King's powder-monkeys.

Hellspite, do you take one up behind you, and Beelzebub the other. But hold on, my sons, for we have some ground to cover and the going must be fast. By the time dawn breaks, you'll at least be not so stiff in the joints as your great bully masters." Then turning to the sailors he added, "And now, my bully tars, let's see how your sea-legs can spring to it ashore." Waving his sword, he pointed across the marsh seawards before breaking into a canter, which was followed by the cavalcade.

As the Press-gang afterwards confessed, the journey to the beach would not have been so long had the Scarecrow led them as the crow would fly. But with devilish ingenuity he stretched the route out to the breaking-point, zig-zagging this way and that. No sooner had they leapt a dyke than the Scarecrow would double back and plunge into it, the muddy water round the sailors' heads, and all the time he kept urging them to greater speed. Jumping, leaping, falling and splashing, the Press-gang's curses dwindled down to moaning, till, torn with brambles, caked with mud, kicked by the flying hoofs, cut by their ropes, and soaked with the cold dyke water, the facetious leader brought them to the endless shingle of Dungeness. Here he called a halt, and while signals were exchanged with flashers to a distant point, the powder-monkeys were allowed to stretch their limbs.

"We'll spare the horses the pebbles," said the Scarecrow. "The boys are waiting for us yonder with the tubs. Escorting party, dismount, and put your back-stays on. We've got to move before the dawn." The men who held the ropes dismounted, as well as ten others who carried pistols. From a hiding-place amongst the scrub-bush some twenty pairs of backstays were produced. These were flat boards, which from time immemorial the dwellers of Dungeness were used to slide over the great pebbles, snow-shoewise, for a long walk there is death to shoe-leather and breaking to the ankles.

Needless to say, the unfortunate Press-gang were not supplied with them.

"The powder-monkeys can stay with us," said the Scarecrow, "while you lads go to help with the tubs. See whether these bully tars are better at the carrying than they have proved themselves at the jumping." The agony of that long tramp through millions of slipping pebbles completed the misery of the sailors. But they had still to find that the Scarecrow had not finished with them. Some forty tub-carriers hoisted their burdens with the ease that came of use. A tub on the chest and a tub on the back, supported by braces of stout webbing, was the method employed by the Scarecrow's carriers, who wore long smocks and blackened their faces with gunpowder. In grade and pay they were the third rankers of his organization. The Night-riders being scaled first, and the boats' crews second.

When the sailors were loaded up with their tubs, they groaned beneath the weight, not knowing that the Scarecrow had ordered twenty tubs to be filled with stones for their especial benefit. To add to their misery and in order that they should not know their destination, they were all blindfolded. When they objected to this, a sprightly little Night-rider called Hellspite replied, "You submit with a good grace, for if I had my way I'd have doused your glims so that you could never squint through a telescope again to spy on honest men." It would have been galling to Stubbard had he recognized this fierce little devil as "the old blasted Sexton Mipps".

After some two hours of being prodded along in the dark, the wretched sailors were utterly exhausted with the weight of the tubs, their constant falls, and the gruelling pace over the roughest ground. At last a halt was called and the tubs were removed. The sailors were then allowed to lie down and rest.

When their bandages were removed they found that they were lying side by side, with their ropes fastened to iron rings in the stone wall of what proved to be a large underground stable. At the far end, at a table lit by two tallow dips in bottles, sat the Scarecrow writing. Behind him two Night-riders were in attendance, and in front stood the two little powder-monkeys.

"And now, my brave lads," said the Scarecrow, addressing them, "you two will be released, in order that you may carry this message to Admiral Troubridge. I will read it to you:

"I have pressed your Press-gang. They are employed in carrying tubs of contraband. When the four Hadleys are restored to their homes, I will return to you the ten sailors. The Hadleys are not smugglers, but at least they are Marshmen, and as such I take their part. On receipt of this message you will have four-and-twenty hours to make up your mind. If the Hadleys are not returned by then, the King's Navy will be short of ten sea-dogs. You must further undertake to see that no more of your Press-gangs come to Romney Marsh. —The Scarecrow."

The boys were then blindfolded and led away, after which the

Scarecrow blew out the tallow dips and left the sailors in the dark.

Although Admiral Troubridge was at first defying the Scarecrow, hoping that Stubbard and his men might effect their escape, the strong opinion on both quarter and lower decks forced him to release the Hadleys, after which they waited in Dover for the reappearance of the Press-gang, no one doubting, except the Admiral, but that the Scarecrow would keep to his side of the bargain.

The next night the Scarecrow's fleet once more put into Dymchurch Bay, and after successfully beating off the Revenue cutter, made good a very profitable landing. But they were not destined to have it all their own way, for one of the smaller luggers tacked too far from her protecting vessels, and the Revenue men were able to cut her off. Seeing danger, and determined at all costs to avoid capture, her crew of four men sprang overboard and swam for the beach, where they had the mortification of seeing their prize of good barrels taken in to by the cutter towards Dover, where they eventually came to anchor in the harbour, the officer putting a couple of armed men aboard the lugger to guard it till morning. Knowing that their officer had not examined the barrels carefully, nor checked up their number, the two guards agreed to broach one of the casks and sample the liquor. With the help of a mallet and a marline-spike they stove in the bung. No sooner had the marline spike gone home than, to their astonishment and terror, a dull moaning issued from the cask, and as though this were not enough to unsettle their nerves, a chorus of gibbering and moaning issued from all the other barrels. It was then that they noticed chalk letters round the barrels, and by the light of a lantern read, "Pressed Press-gang returned for duty, with the Scarecrow's compliments." After giving the alarm, the casks were opened, and each contained one of the gagged Press-gang. Ten miserable, half-suffocated sailors.

When the news spread to Dymchurch, Doctor Syn looked at Sexton Mipps and chuckled. "I'm relieved to think that the rascals have gone back to duty alive. I had no fear that they would suffocate, and as the barrels were warped and let in sufficient air; but I suffered some qualms about the lugger. She had got so cursedly unseaworthy that I was afraid she might let in enough water to drown the rascals, and I had no wish to send them to their deaths. We are well rid of the old lugger, though."

"Aye," returned Mipps. "She was past repair, and I doubt if she'd have weathered another cross-Channel trip."

"I'd like to have seen the unpacking of that Stubbard," laughed the Vicar.

"Poor devil. Suppose you open a bottle of brandy, Mipps, so that we can drink the like damnation to all our enemies."

Chapter 20. The black list paid

Throughout Romney Marsh, on any night when a big "run" was to go forward, it was a noticeable thing that a rough chalk drawing of a scarecrow would appear upon the many stable doors that harboured good horses, whether hunters, shires or ponies. Upon seeing this, the stablemen, whose duty it was to lock up for the night, either did not lock up or left the key in a place were the unknown Night-riders could find it. Certain horses might be spared, though these were few enough, and to mark this favouritism a chalk cross would mysteriously appear upon the post of the animal's stall. One animal that could always boast a cross was the fat pony belonging to the Vicar of Dymchurch, Doctor Syn.

"Open your stable doors tonight," was a familiar whisper upon Romney Marsh.

On a certain evening in midsummer, a long string of gipsy caravans wended their way slowly along the winding Marsh road. They were all of the tribe Pettigrand, a name held in high honour amongst their race. They were led by old Silas Pettigrand, the patriarchal head of the tribe. He rode his horse bareback, letting the rope that served as rein hang loose upon the animal's neck.

A grave, gaunt figure, this Silas, as with long beard and far-seeing eyes, hawk-nose and long upright body, he seemed part of the horse on which he rode.

Leading the way, he turned off from the road into a large stretch of meadowland known in Dymchurch as the Fair Field, where he gave signal to draw in and pitch camp.

While the men of the tribe busied themselves with their horses and firebuilding, and the women set about preparing the night meal, old Silas approached one of his many sons and nodded towards a bridge that spanned a broad dyke on the far side of the camp. Leaning against the parapet of this Tudor brick bridge were three men.

The younger gipsy noticed the deep frown that spread upon his chief's face as he muttered, "My son, the carrion are here already." As gravely as his father, the son replied with a smile that had to it no vestige of humour, but rather of deep respect. "You have still the sharp eyes, my father."

306_ _"Not sharp enough to read their faces, though, at this distance," replied Silas. "Can you?" The son nodded. "They appear to be amused at something."

"And when the Tankerton brothers are amused," went on the father, "it generally means that they have spied something to their own advantage. Let us go and see if we can discover what it is." Slowly he walked across the Fair Field followed by his son. The Tankerton brothers were half-bred gipsies, and had no love for any of the Pettigrands, but as Silas came near they gave him the welcome, "Good tenting." To this Silas replied, "and free from horse-thieves and other evils, we hope." The three laughed, and one of them said: "Every man to his trade. You buy horses, old man, and sell them at good profit. If other men can get horses without purchase, and yet sell them to advantage, you should not grudge them their better fortune. Whenever we get the good luck to see an animal straying, out of our good nature we do our best to find it a good home. Is there so much evil in that?"

"It is evil to cut a picketing rope in order that an animal shall stray," returned Silas. "I have come to warn you not to enter our camp circle; for we prefer to find homes for our horses ourselves. Knowing well that the Tankertons prefer riding to walking, I keep my eyes the wider open when I meet them afoot." Again the Tankertons laughed, and another of them replied: "There are other horses than those of the Pettigrands in these parts, and we are not after yours. It amuses us, though, to see that someone else is after them. No doubt you will close your wide-open eyes when his horse-borrowers appear. Look." The half-breed pointed to the brick wall on the opposite side of the little bridge, and Silas saw the rough chalk drawing of a scarecrow.

"When the Scarecrow borrows he pays back with good interest," retorted Silas. "And with such I am ever willing to trade. But even for profit I do not allow my people to trade with a Tankerton. My men have also instructions to deal roughly with horse thieves, so again I tell you to keep clear of the Fair Field while our caravans are on it."

"You cannot close the right of way upon the Marsh bridges, old man," sneered the third Tankerton. "Neither can you frighten us with your threats. We are going now, not to humour you, but because we have some pressing business elsewhere. And may the Scarecrow return the horses which he will borrow from you, for should he at any time fail to do so there will be a great squealing from the Pettigrands." And with this final retort the horse-thieves slouched over the bridge and set their faces towards the village of

Dymchurch.

The Tankertons spent their evening drinking in the village taverns and talking amongst themselves. But they listened too, though the scraps of conversation which they overheard seemed harmless enough and failed to teach them what they were trying to find out. At last, however, there came into the bar parlour of the Ship Inn the quizzical little sexton of Dymchurch, Mr. Mipps.

The Tankertons watched him closely from their corner, and saw him cross over to a farm labourer who was leaning against the bar.

"Good evening, George," they heard him say. "I owe you a good pint, I think, for you see you was right and I was wrong. That there haystack what we saw afire was not at Black's place but at Botolph's Bridge."

"Aye, at Botolph's Bridge," returned George.

"Botolph's Bridge it is, George," echoed Mipps, "and what's more it will go on burning till midnight, for the lazy old Ted ain't the man to leave his tankard for to put out a fire if I knows him."

"We'll have one more, brothers, and then get along," said the eldest Tankerton.

"Have you found it out then?" asked the second brother, when they got outside.

"I have," nodded his elder.

"How on earth?" asked the youngest, "for I never heard nothing."

"Aye, because that sexton is cautious on behalf of the smugglers," explained the eldest. "No one will ever catch that little rat unless an officer of the Crown comes along with as much brain as me, which I take it ain't likely. I puts two and two together, and the answer comes out very much four as I sees it.

Through information received like, I knows that George Betts is the best hand with horses around Dymchurch. He can keep a bunch of wild 'uns tame 'cos he's got the way with 'em, see? He's one of the Scarecrow's horse-holders consequently. Therefore when Mipps comes in and says all that nonsense about a burning rick, I looks out for a message and watches for the words to be laid on, see? Well, I gets Botolph's Bridge, and that's the place you can lay to it where he's to be waiting to take over the Night-riders' horses, so that they can lend a hand with loading the pack ponies. And I gets the time, too, midnight, and for want of better information I suggests that we get along to Botolph's Bridge and spy out the land, as it were."

Doctor Syn walked slowly from the church towards the Vicarage, talking quietly to his sexton. The parish beadle came out of the Court House as they passed and remarked to the Vicar that he considered it would be a fine night.

"And glad I am of it too," he added. "When it's wet I finds I has to tuck up my shirt collar, and that interferes with my hearing, which is dangerous when all them wild foreign Egyptians is encamped in the Fair Field. Far be it from me to question the Squire, but why he lets them folk stay about the village buying and selling horses I don't know."

The Vicar laughed. "Why, my good Mr. Beadle, there's nothing wrong with the Pettigrands. They keep to themselves and behave themselves very properly.

Old Silas looks after his people, just as the Squire looks after us." The beadle shook his head and pointed to the gallows outside the Court House.

"If I had my way I'd have all them Egyptians strung up yonder," he said.

"With all respects to you opinion, Vicar, I thinks thieving's in their blood, and they sells horses that they never buy."

"Some of them, perhaps," replied Doctor Syn, "but not the Pettigrands."

"You thinks everyone's as honest and good as yourself, sir," said the beadle.

"But for all that, being beadle, and responsible for the safety of the parish, I'm going to warn the village that Egyptians is in our midst, and to look to their property. Good night, Vicar."

"He gives me a good character, Mipps," said Syn with a chuckle, as the beadle walked away. "And now you had better saddle up my pony, for it is time for me to be starting across the Marsh. Also get word to Jimmie Bone that he must meet me at the secret stable a quarter of an hour sooner than we said.

That applies to you as well. I've heard that a troop of Dragoons are to be out tonight, and I am in the mind to give them a race. Our three horses are in good fettle, and I think the gallant soldiers will follow us if we break away from the rest. They would rather capture the Scarecrow and his lieutenants, Hellspite and Beelzebub, than all the tubs in Smuggledom." With a nod, Doctor Syn passed on to the front door of the Vicarage, while Mipps went to the stable and saddled up the parson's sturdy little white pony.

At the same time, Silas Pettigrand was making his final inspection of the gipsy camp before retiring to his own caravan.

"You will keep the strictest watch for the Tankerton thieves," he ordered his sons. "Whoever is on watch and sees a glimpse of them, rouse the camp. But when you hear three hoots of an owl, followed by the cry of a curlew, turn your backs upon the picketing lines till the Scarecrow's men have taken what horses they need." Old Silas did not realize that for once the Tankertons had spoken truth.

They had a better plan than attempting a raid upon the camp. They were waiting for the Night-riders' horses at Botolph's Bridge.

For some hours they lay concealed, grasping their thick cudgels. About midnight they heard firing at sea, for the Revenue cutter was being driven off by the smuggling fleet, and then in the silence that followed came the sound of horses along the road. Some dozen riders in all, dressed as Marsh Witches, and, much to the satisfaction of the Tankertons, all were mounted well. They drew rein and waited by the bridge, while the robbers watched them from the ambush of a deep dry dyke.

Presently there arose in the silence of the night three hoots of an owl, and then the plaintive cry of a curlew. Upon this signal the party dismounted, and after handing over their reins to two of their party the other ten walked along the road to meet a string of pack ponies that were making their way towards the beach.

"They're not risking losing these horses to the Dragoons," whispered the eldest Tankerton.

The horse-holders sat on the ground facing their charges, and with their backs to the Tankertons, who very quietly crept from the dyke and crawled towards them. Two sickening cracks from the cruel cudgels and the Nightriders were senseless. Though the horses shied, the Tankertons were quickly in the saddle, and each with three led horses they galloped away in the opposite direction to that taken by the smugglers, leaving their victims behind them, dead for all they cared.

Meanwhile three horsemen rode out of the woods at Lympne and drew rein, listening.

"We've shaken off the rascals," said the Scarecrow. "I thought our doubling back through the wood would do the business." As his two lieutenants nodded, a bright light shot up in the sky.

"And there goes the beacon on Aldington Knoll. That means the tubs are landed, packed and off to the hides in Dungeness. We can now ride down to the sea-wall and dismiss the others." Saying which the Scarecrow and his companions rode down the hill to the Marsh. When they reached the sea-wall, ten dismounted witches rose to meet them.

"All clear, Scarecrow," they muttered.

"Then get back to the bridge as quick as you may, get mounted and ride like hell for home. The dawn will be on us soon," and the Scarecrow and his two mounted men rode off for the hidden stables.

An hour later Doctor Syn, having seen to his pony, closed the Vicarage door and, after a copious drink of brandy, mounted the stairs for bed. Half way up he stopped and listened, for in the garden had arisen the hooting of an owl. This was followed by a gentle scratching at the hall casement. He went down and opened the door, admitting Mipps and, much to the Doctor's astonishment, Silas Pettigrand.

"The boys found the horse-holders senseless at Botolph's, Vicar," gasped the out-of-breath sexton. "The horses were gone. The boys, suspecting the Pettigrands, searched the camp. No sign of the horses, and old Silas here accounted for all his men. No one had left camp."

"It is the Tankertons," said Silas, and he told the Vicar of his encounter with them. "You are my friend and brother. Whether you come to me as Doctor Syn or the Scarecrow I would never betray you."

"I know it," replied Syn, grasping the old man's hand. "I trust you. But others will not. The Scarecrow cannot ride after the thieves now, for the dawn is upon us, but for your sake as well as mine, let one of your people ride on the rascals' track and find out where they are bound, and tomorrow night the Scarecrow's men will ride after them."

"I will send two of my sons," replied the gipsy. "They will find them, and while one keeps watch the other can return with news."

"Then go quickly," ordered Doctor Syn. "No doubt the rogues will ride across the Kent Ditch, and hide in Sussex till they can sell the horses. And may your sons have good hunting."

"They will find them," said the old man as he went out into the dawn.

The following morning a notice was fixed to the gallows post outside the Court House:

The Scarecrow regrets to inform such as it may concern, that while my Night-riders were busy landing a most goodly supply of contraband last night, two of my horse-holders were set upon by villains and their charges driven away. I pledge you my word of honour that you will not be losers, for I shall make it my business to recover the stolen cattle. I will also hand over the thieves to be tried at our Court House for the heinous crime of horse-stealing.

When the beadle discovered that two of the Pettigrand men were missing, he took old Silas into custody. Doctor Syn, however, went to the Squire, and after some difficulty obtained his release from the cell. Thus it was that the gipsy was able to bring Doctor Syn news later in the day that the horse thieves were in hiding at a deserted farm across the Kent Ditch which they were planning to vacate as soon as darkness fell. Meanwhile Silas's son would follow them and leave gipsy signs behind him for his people to pick up.

Not wishing to lose his own valuable horses, which were amongst those missing, the Squire saw to it that no steps were taken to embarrass the mysterious Scarecrow in the fulfilling of his promise, and so it happened that after darkness had fallen a large body of Night-riders were galloping across the Marsh for the border.

Under the same darkness the Tankertons also set out, never suspecting that they had been trailed by one of the hated Pettigrands. Although hampered by their led horses, they made good pace. But the pace of the Scarecrow's Legion was faster, and at a lonely part of the road between Rye and Winchelsea they were charged before and behind by the Scarecrow's Demon Riders. With the fear of death upon them, when they realized who it was that had them in his power, they were bound upon the stolen horses, face downwards and facing the horse's tail. In this manner they were brought back ignominiously to Dymchurch.

It was the beadle who discovered them, for, waking up in the dawn by the continual hooting of an owl, he opened his casement and saw three horses tied to rings in the wall beneath him, and upon their backs lay three bound men more dead than alive. The same dawn discovered the remaining stolen animals peacefully standing in their accustomed stalls.

The trial of the Tankertons was a great sensation in the neighbourhood. Sir Antony Cobtree, presiding, took a serious and hard line of action, so that despite Doctor Syn's urging clemency, the jury, in support of the Squire's summing up, found the brothers guilty. They were to be made an example, and hanged from the Dymchurch gallows.

The night before the execution Doctor Syn sat drinking with Sexton Mipps in the Vicarage study.

"Even in our hardest days, old friend," he said, "I think you will own that I used clemency wherever possible. The wretches that we made to walk the plank aboard the old ship deserved their deaths far more than these wretched horse thieves. Yet we spared when we could, and often at the risk of our own safety."

"That's right, sir," agreed Mipps. "But you can do no more for those men.

You have pleaded, and it's no good." Doctor Syn smiled. "But suppose the Scarecrow rescued them? I think it would cause a sensation, and a valuable one at that. Where does the beadle keep the keys of the cell at night?"

"He carries 'em up to bed with him," replied Mipps.

"Then saddle my pony, for the Scarecrow is going to rescue them." Three hours later the grim figure of the Scarecrow was standing upon his horse's back immediately beneath the casement where the beadle slept. He awoke hearing a raucous whisper ordering him to get out of bed and hand over the cell keys. The sight of the levelled horse pistol persuaded him to obey.

"And if you attempt to leave your house before the dawn you will be shot by one of my men who is watching your door from the churchyard wall. I am not having the prisoners hanged tomorrow morning. I have decided to deal with them myself." Two minutes later the wretched prisoners were as terrified as the beadle had been when the Scarecrow entered the cell and ordered them to walk out quietly.

Outside Mipps, dressed as Hellspite, waited with three horses, which they were ordered to mount. They rode to the beach, where a fishing boat was waiting for the tide to carry the Scarecrow's orders to France. Here they were ordered into the cabin and shut in.

When the sun rose and the first of the crowd began collecting to get good places for the execution, a notice was found fastened to the gallows:

There will be no hanging. I have decided to punish these Tankertons myself.

The Scarecrow.

And as Mipps remarked to the Vicar that night over their brandy: "There's no one in the neighbourhood or out of it what don't think the old Scarecrow ain't a perfect marvel. And so say I, and here's to you, sir." Doctor Syn's reply to that was, "Pass me the black book, Mipps, for I believe that with our settlement against these Tankertons our debts are paid." Mipps unlocked the iron chest and handed his master the sinister volume.

"Well, Vicar, there's no doubt but that all these names what you wrote in it has caused us a coffin-load of trouble."

"Excitement as well," replied the Vicar. "Come, my good Mipps, you must allow them credit for giving us some exciting adventures."

"Well, we've finished with 'em now for a bit," said Mipps, "and p'r'aps we can enjoy a nice little bit of anchorage. Go ashore, as it were, sir, for a bit and spend our profits."

"Not quite yet, I think, for there is still a name here to be dealt with, my good Mipps."

"Who's that then?" asked the sexton.

Doctor Syn, whose thin fingers had been turning over the pages of the black book, suddenly closed the clasps with a snap as he answered, "The Archbishop."

"Oh, leave him alone," urged Mipps. "There's not much fun in mucking about with an Archbishop."

"But he was a proscribed enemy, my good Mipps," went on the Vicar.

"Perhaps you have forgotten the very rude and personal things he said about the Scarecrow in his sermon."

"No, he laid it on think, I confess," admitted Mipps. "But let's leave the old grumbletonian alone."

"Perhaps you have forgotten my comment at the time."

"No, I never forgets nothing what you says, sir. It don't pay to forget them things, I've found."

"Then what did I say?" asked the Vicar.

"Why, you thought of taking him along to repeat his sermon to the Nightriders. But he'd never do it, not proper. He'd turn it all milk-and-watery."

"Not if the Scarecrow ordered otherwise," replied Syn. "Oh, and it would be vastly amusing. Most diverting, on my soul. Think of it, Mipps. Think of removing His Grace, night-gowned and night-capped, from his bed in Canterbury Palace, mounting him on Gehenna in front of the Scarecrow, and then galloping through the narrow echoing streets and out into the country along Stone Street. Think of meeting the Night-riders at Slippery Sam's, then on and down to the Marsh for the sermon." Mipps grinned. "Yes, sir. Very funny if you looks at it in that way. But there's two sides to everything, even a joke."

"And what's the other side to this joke?" asked Syn. "The Archbishop's discomfort?"

"No, sir. The Night-riders'. What have they gone and done that they should be inflicted with the Archbishop's sermon all over again?"

"Aye, Mipps, there is that way of looking at it," sighed Syn. "Well, then we'll leave His Grace alone and pass the brandy." And as he took the bottle from the sexton, Syn began to sing quietly Clegg's old chanty:

Oh, here's to the feet what have walked the plank; Yo-ho for the Dead Man's Throttle.

Mipps grinned again. "I believe you hankers to be Clegg again."

"Well, who knows, my good little Mipps, but that even yet it may not be cut and run for us, and another spell of piracy upon the high seas.

So here's to the corpses afloat in the Tank, and the Dead Man's teeth in the Bottle."